Saving Angel

A NOVEL

By
Glenn Morris

Bainbridge Editions

Boston New York Paris

Published by
Bainbridge Editions
A division of
Eli Bainbridge and Company, Inc.
33 Murray Road
West Newton, Massachusetts 02465
855.556.5561
646.405.5280 (NYC)
33.1.70.38.73.20 (Paris)

www.bainbridgeeditions.com

The characters and events in this book are fictitious. Any simi-
larity to real persons, living or dead, is coincidental and not
intended by the author.

ISBN: 1939772028
ISBN 13: 9781939772022

For Isabelle

In order of appearance, major characters in **bold**:

Carol LaPierre, Bursar, Boston Institute for Architecture

Ramone Cortes, Student, Boston Institute for Architecture

Ben Holt, Architect and majority owner, Satart Holt Architects; Husband of Claudine Aubrey Holt; Father of Daniel, Pascal (Pasha), Emma and Abeille; Chair of the Board at Boston Institute for Architecture

Claudine Aubrey Holt, Fashion Designer; Wife of Ben Holt; Mother of Daniel, Pascal (Pasha), Emma and Abeille; Daughter of Marcel and Bernadine Aubrey

Robert, Ben and Claudine's major domo; Babette's husband

Daniel Holt, Ben and Claudine's eldest son; Simone's boyfriend

Pascal (Pascha) Holt, Ben and Claudine's son and second eldest child

Emma Holt, Ben and Claudine's daughter and third eldest child

The Black Suburban, a very large armored SUV, actually one of several that play the character

Marcel Aubrey, Wealthy French industrialist, Claudine's father, Bernadine's husband

Marc Lipoff, Newton Massachusetts politician and Boston bank executive

Hezekiah Wilson (Zeke), Architect, former classmate of Ben Holt, new member of Boston Institute for Architecture Board

Munroe Owen Sather, Architect; member of Boston Institute for Architecture Board; Partner in Brown, Campbell and Sather

Angel Piscara, Dean of the Boston Institute for Architecture; old friend of Pascal Satart

George Theroux, President of the Boston Institute for Architecture

Emma Pittsfield, Piscara's secretary

Cheryl, Secretary at Brown, Campbell and Sather

Isabel Deschamps, Physician and Claudine's doctor

The Mayor, Mayor of the City of Newton, Massachusetts

Jim Britton, Jimmy Mullane and Jim Barry, Department Heads, City of Newton Massachusetts

Liz Hatchett, Annie Hatchett's daughter

Annie Hatchett, Nurse, high school girlfriend of Ben Holt, Liz Hatchett's mother

Diane Hanley, Annie Hatchett's best friend in high school, Josh Hanley's wife

Josh Hanley, Medical Researcher, Diane Hanley's husband

Jared Whiting, Architect and senior staff at Satart Holt, one of Ben Holt's first friends in Paris

Simone, Daniel Holt's girlfriend

Pascal Satart, Architect and Partner in Satart Holt; Friend of Angel Piscara and Marcel Aubrey

Severine Fontaine Satart, Architect, Pascal Satart's wife

Bill Button, shadowy former CIA agent; some sort of consultant to shadowy U. S. Government agencies; some sort of friend of Ben Holt; Husband of Rachel Button; Father of Amélie Button

Gunter Steuben, Ben and Claudine Holt's head of security; Master of the Black Suburbans

Babette, Ben and Claudine Holt's cook, Robert's wife

Carlos Y, Wealthy shadowy businessman in Rio de Janiero, Former Colombian drug king (reformed?), Father of Carlos Y (the son)

Doug Strout, Ben Holt's investigator, advisor and confidant; former bodyguard for Marine Corps generals; former CIA trainer

Bernadine Aubrey, Marcel Aubrey's wife; Claudine holt's mother; ran shadowy insurance company and investment bank in Bermuda; presumed dead after plane carrying her and piloted by Rachel Button was lost at sea. (See *Obligation for Justice*)

Abeille Claudine Holt, Ben and Claudine's daughter and the baby

Gene, Medical investor and friend of Ben Holt

Anton Vasilevich Dashkov, Russian real estate developer and gangster; former low-level gangster in Russian mob

Stoekl, Dashkov's right-hand man

Blair Winston, Marcel's attorney, Ben's attorney

Carl Specks, Attorney for Mo Sather

Ellsworth Nelson, Architecture critic for the Boston Post

Josep Rufi, Head of Staff at Satart Holt Architects, Paris office

Peter Pepper, Member of Boston Institute for Architecture Board

Andy Berman, Member of Boston Institute for Architecture Board, BIA Alumni President

Carlos Y, the son of Carlos Y

Paul Hogan, Architect and senior staff at Satart Holt, one of Ben Holt's first friends in Paris

Judge Brian Wilcox, Massachusetts Superior Court Judge

Tony Ramp, Newton Corner Neighborhood Association Chair

Gilles, Guard at the Fondation Bernadine Aubrey

Carmen Ortega, U. S. Attorney for Boston

Simon Pierce, U. S. Treasury agent

Frank Leahy, Carmen Ortega's First Assistant U. S. Attorney

Tim Morris, Criminal defense attorney representing Ben Holt

Carl Blass, U. S Treasury agent, Simon Pierce's boss

Spider, CIA National Clandestine Service agent in deep cover

Lorraine, Bookkeeper at Satart Holt Architects, Paris office

Peter and Gustav, Staff at Satart Holt, Paris office

1

THE BOY SITTING ACROSS THE BREAKFAST TABLE FROM Carol was dark and handsome but so, she thought, were they all. She liked the way his curly black hair was cut tight to his head. His muscles were tight too, not so large as to be a caricature but well defined. Carol especially liked his broad biceps. They were, she thought, his sexy muscle. "Listen, " she said to him. "I've got to go have a mammogram and get my hair done. I'll drop you at the trolley."

She wondered how long he would keep his tight abs, his lean face, his hair. He was twenty-seven, so with a little luck he might have ten years. They wouldn't though. He had lasted longer than most. Having sat in her office at the Boston Institute for Architecture filling out his student loan application six days ago, he had gone home with her that night.

She wished she could remember his name—it was an "R" name, she thought. She made a mental note to look it up in his records.

BEN SAW CLAUDINE as he walked into their bedroom. She was lying on her back on the floor by the tall windows, her knees raised over her hips, her toes pointed at Ben. She lifted her hips and rolled over, now facing the floor with her knees tucked under her chest, her arms extended to her feet and her palms facing the ceiling.

I

"Does your back still hurt?" he said.

Claudine uncoiled and rose in one smooth motion, stretching to her full height, her hands now reaching for the ceiling. "Yes, and the yoga only helps for a short time."

"When are you going to see the doctor?"

"Not until after the shows are over. I don't have the time and I can't afford to lose my concentration."

"And then you'll put it off until after the Springwear shows, then until the couture shows are over."

Claudine wrapped her long, lithe arms around Ben's neck and pulled his face close to hers. She bit his lower lip and, as he recoiled, kissed the lip that she had just punished. "Let's not argue about this Ben. I'm fine—just working too hard."

"Okay. I just hate seeing you hurt."

"If I thought that a doctor would help I'd go. Now, let's gather everyone and start the day."

ROBERT WAS AT his usual morning post in the foyer. He was a tall, elegant man who reminded Ben of Giscard D'Estaing in stature and manner, although Claudine claimed she couldn't see it.

As Claudine and Ben descended the stairs, Daniel joined the butler with Pascha close behind him. Ben surveyed the faces of his two sons—Daniel had Ben's square face and bushy eyebrows, Pascha had Claudine's long neck and turned-up nose.

"Where's Emma?" asked Ben.

"I'm behind you, Da-dee. Quiet as a church mouse."

Ben smiled, remembering the story that they had read at bedtime the night before. "We're a bit early. Shall we walk Claudine to work before we walk to school?"

"May we, Mama?" Emma begged.

"Yes. Today, but don't plan on it being every day."

As the troupe walked out the door, Robert pulled a walkie-talkie from an inside pocket of his jacket. "Gunter, change of plans this morning…"

AS BEN EMERGED onto the sidewalk with Claudine's arm in his, the headlights of a black Suburban across the narrow street flashed. The headlights on a black Mercedes sedan at the next intersection flashed a response. Seeing the "all-clear" signal, the family headed toward Rue de Bac on the way to Claudine's atelier. Daniel and Pascha walked ahead, dressed in black suits, Pascha now almost as tall as Daniel. Claudine followed with Emma's hand in her free hand. By the end of the block, Ben slipped out of Claudine's grasp to follow behind and watch Claudine walk, looking for signs of her back pain.

CAROL PULLED TO the curb at the Bus Stop sign and turned her face to the boy in the passenger seat. He leaned in to kiss her just as she turned her head towards the meter maid, who was gesturing wildly at her out the window. His kiss landed on her neck and he recoiled in embarrassment. She just smiled at him. She liked the attention of her young men, and there had been many. Perhaps it was her magnificent blonde, chin-length bob with blunt bangs; her nose that could have been made for her but was her own; or her short trim body with breasts that attracted attention but stopped short of buxom.

"You'll have to jump out before she writes me a ticket," she said.

"Will I see you tonight?"

"Go!"

The boy stepped out of the car and eyed the meter maid. She leered back at him. The leer made him decide against a confrontation. He crossed in front of the car, almost being hit by a bicycle messenger, and trotted to the trolley stop in the median of the roadway. As the meter maid approached the driver's side, Carol lowered the window. "Good morning, Shirley."

"Carol. Another one of your toys?"

"Gotta go—a bus is coming," Carol called through the window as she pulled on the power switch and the window slid closed.

"I'll call you tonight," Shirley called back as Carol pulled away.

2

WITH THE CONSTRUCTION AT OCEAN PARK WIND-
ing down, Marcel, Ben and the investors made arrangements
to refinance the project and retained U.S. Trust of Boston to arrange
the financing. Their mortgage banker, Marc Lipoff, had secured financing for several large projects in the Boston area and throughout New
England, but he had not financed anything like the small city that
Ocean Park had become. Few had. Despite the unique character of the
project, Lipoff successfully arranged a buy-out of equity in a few short
months. The return on investment exceeded anyone's expectations
and the investors were elated. Ben was a bit melancholy; he would no
longer have any ownership position in the development other than his
penthouse condominium. It was a story he should be familiar with:
Every architecture project is birthed by the designer, and every designer coddles that project into fruition—only to have to turn the keys over
to an adoptive parent when the project is done.

But this story was different. Ocean Park was Ben's last real connection to the city he'd grown up in, and, he realized, the last connection
to the places he'd shared with his late brother, Don. His mother and
father had both passed in the last few years; his brother Ron had moved
to Manchester-by-the-Sea, and his sister Jen had moved to Arizona with
her husband. Ben sensed that he would be visiting the condominium
less frequently than he'd thought when he'd had it added to the top of
the tallest building in the complex.

The night before the papers were to be signed, Ben sat in front of the two-story tall windows with the lights off and looked out at the lighted crane tower that had been converted into the Don Holt Memorial Winter Garden.

AFTER THE PAPERS for the sale of equity were signed, Lipoff approached Ben. Lipoff was short, with nearly black curly hair that grayed at the temples. His skin seemed perpetually tanned, but showed not a wrinkle. He looked like someone who had spent too much time in the sun or under a lamp. "Congratulations, Ben. You created something wonderful, and you and Marcel have made a small fortune off of it."

"Thanks, Marc." Ben reached out and laid his hand on Marc's shoulder. "You did a great job with the equity placement. I think I could get the investors to put up money for almost anything we want to do next, although I saw that a couple of them are looking at yacht brokers' brochures. I'd better sign them up before they spend everything they've made."

"Well, I may have something for you." Marc went on to tell Ben that he was heavily involved in the politics of a city next to Boston—Newton, Massachusetts. He was a former alderman and was very close to its long-time mayor. He went on to describe a project—actually a series of four or five projects—that he wanted to take on there.

He described Newton as a city made up of thirteen villages, each with a unique character. The villages made Newton—one of the larger cities in Massachusetts—into a wonderfully livable community with strong local identity. Lipoff's description intrigued Ben and he listened intently.

The Massachusetts Turnpike had been extended from a circumferential highway into the heart of downtown Boston. Newton lay along the new highway's path and three out of four of the villages that lay across its patch were dissected by the road. Two of them—Newton Corner and Newtonville—were ripped into two separate parts each, north and south, and the wide, depressed highway made pedestrian travel between them uncomfortable. Lipoff wanted to stitch the villages back together again with developments over the turnpike.

They agreed to meet when Ben was next back in Boston for a BIA board meeting.

"Ben, I have to tell you that most people I know would love to stay in Paris and forget Boston."

"I know, Marc. When Thomas Wolfe wrote that you can't go home again, he apparently wasn't talking about me. I can never seem to stop coming home. I come home to Boston, then I turn around and come home to Paris. It sounds like a *Twilight Zone* episode."

Marc laughed, then turned and walked away, shaking his head.

3

THE BOSTON INSTITUTE FOR ARCHITECTURE BOARD met in the school's Memorial Library, which had been relocated intact from its original location on Boston's Beacon Hill. The dark wood shelves were populated with old leather and cloth bound volumes, many of them monographs bearing the names of the famous architects and firms that had founded the school more than a hundred years earlier.

Ben sat in the middle of the long side of the heavily detailed oak table. He remembered the days when he would sneak into this room late on a Saturday night and spread out the rolled tracing paper on which he would draw for many long hours. He remembered the smell of the room—mold and mildew and furniture polish—and noted how it was now joined by the smell of the toner emanating from the recently added copy machine.

Hezekiah Wilson, Ben's former classmate, entered the room and raised his heavily filled, well-worn leather satchel onto the table. Wilson's hair was still full and moppish, but was now completely gray and joined by an equally bushy gray mustache. "Ben," he said. "It's good to see you."

Ben rose to greet him. "It's great to see you, Zeke. I'm looking forward to your being on the board."

"Thanks." Wilson opened his satchel and withdrew a brown paper bag. He set it on the table and flattened it, then withdrew a waxed-paper wrapped sandwich from his satchel and placed it on the bag. "Want some, Ben? It's ham and cheese."

"No thanks, Zeke. I ate on the way."

AS SEVERAL OF the BIA Board members started to arrive, Ben got up from his seat and moved to the end of the table at the far end of the room opposite the door. Most of the arriving members greeted Ben, then introduced themselves to Wilson before taking a seat and engaging in conversation with other Board members in groups of two or three.

One of the last to arrive, accompanied by two other Board members, was Munroe Sather. He moved to the center of the table where Wilson was sitting alone—an empty chair on either side of him—and offered his hand. "Munroe Owen Sather."

Wilson hadn't seen Sather since his days as a student. Sather had become thinner, almost gaunt, but had otherwise aged little. He still carried an arrogant fire in his steel blue eyes. "Hezekiah Wilson, Mister Sather."

"So you're the new boy."

"Yes, sir, I suppose I am."

"Would you kindly move to another chair, Wilson. Preferably to a seat near the door."

Wilson noticed that the sentence was delivered as a declaration—not a request. He moved to a corner seat near the door and then, remembering his satchel, returned to recover it.

The stooped figure of Angel Piscara—his pure white hair protruding from the edges of his black beret—entered the room.

Wilson rose to greet him, offering his hand. "Good evening, Dean."

"Ah, Wilson. Good to have you with us."

"Thank you, Dean, I..."

Piscara patted Wilson's shoulder, but didn't stop, continuing along the row of chairs toward the head of the table. He moved through the room slowly, but without hesitation, half-raising his left hand in greeting to each Board member as he passed. At the end of the table, he moved behind Ben and sat in the chair to Ben's left. As Piscara sat down, Ben slid a single piece of paper in front of him and called the meeting to order. His opening words were barely out of his mouth when Carol LaPierre entered the room and sat in a chair directly behind Wilson. She looked directly at Ben and silently mouthed the words, "Sorry I'm late." She took out her steno pad and started writing in shorthand. In the morning, she would turn her notes into meeting minutes.

AFTER AN HOUR-AND-A-HALF board meeting during which reports by the Chair, the President and the treasurer were presented and reports by each of the board committees were made, Ben said, "Hearing no objection, we will be in executive session." He looked around the table. No one spoke.

"Will the staff and observers please excuse us," Ben said. "Except President Theroux and Dean Piscara?"

A dozen people got up and left the room, a few of them stopping to whisper in Sather's ear.

Sather nodded, then spoke. "I would remind the chair that an executive session should not include staff except to make specific limited reports on the matters before the session. I object to the Dean's presence in these..."

Ben replied impatiently, "Mister Sather, it is the Chair's prerogative to invite advisors to executive sessions who can aid the discussion at hand. Unless you intend to make a motion to the Board to over-rule me, a motion that would require a two-thirds vote, your objection is duly noted and rejected. We will proceed with the Dean present."

Sather stared at Ben for a full thirty seconds while no one moved, or—it seemed—breathed. Ben met Sather's stare, finally speaking without breaking eye contact. "Mister Sather, do you have a matter to present?"

"No." Sather pushed away from the table, looked to three of the other Board members opposite him, and then rose.

Ben said. "This meeting is adjourned." He turned to the Dean, "Am I giving you a ride home?"

"Yes, Holt."

4

A FTER CAROL LEFT THE MEETING, SHE WENT BACK TO her office. This was her normal routine. She would wait for Theroux to return to see whether the part of the meeting she missed would impact her job, especially whether the Board had addressed a proposal that Theroux had intended to make limiting financial aid. Emma Pittsfield, the Dean's elderly secretary, would be waiting at her desk just outside the Dean's office, since she never left until he did. Carol and Missus Pittsfield would then leave together, Carol walking part of the way to the MBTA station with the older woman before crossing the street to the garage and her car. If the weather was particularly bad, she would give Missus Pittsfield a ride home.

Tonight, when Theroux returned, he could barely keep up with Sather. He was followed by three of the Board members who were widely mocked as "Sather's Serf's." They almost never spoke at Board meetings and always voted with Sather. The parade marched into Theroux's office. Carol watched Sather hold the office door while the others filed in, then fling the door hard against the jamb behind them. She heard the loud retort and looked to Missus Pittsfield for a reaction. Missus Pittsfield didn't seem to notice.

IT WAS WIDELY known that Monroe Sather was among a group of Boston architects who wanted the BIA to merge with a larger college. The proponents of the merger spoke of expanded resources and opportunities for students and faculty, although it was unclear to the students and faculty what those resources and opportunities might be. Both the student union and the faculty association voted against studying a merger, but the BIA Board kept the matter in limbo, not wanting to vote against the bloc of large firms represented by Sather, but afraid to go against the students and faculty—and the Dean.

The Dean, in fact, had never spoken publicly against the proposal, but his refusal to actively support it was seen as opposition. He had spoken a very few words to no more than three directors—the three oldest members of the Board. He had never asked Ben Holt to oppose consideration of a merger, but was well aware of Ben's distaste for Sather. In any case, he didn't think he needed Ben's vote. He thought he could rely on nine votes on the seventeen-member board: His three cronies and the two representatives each of the students, the faculty and the alumni.

CAROL SAW THE Dean return with Ben. The Dean silently handed Missus Pittsfield a small sheaf of papers and walked into his office, returning almost immediately with his coat, which he struggled into with Ben's help. He raised his black beret to his head and made a small motion with his left hand to Missus Pittsfield.

Ben stopped in front of Emma Pittsfield's desk, looked directly into her face and smiled. "Good night, Missus Pittsfield."

"Good night, Mister Holt. Thank you for taking care of the Dean." She didn't look at Ben while she spoke, which gave him the opportunity to study her face. It was gravely wrinkled with long vertical lines that ran from below her eyes down her cheeks, continuing along her neck until they disappeared beyond the small bow at the collar of her crisply starched white shirt. Her skin nearly matched the shirt; her white hair was only slightly grayer.

SEEING THE DEAN go, Carol knew that Missus Pittsfield would be ready to leave in a few minutes. She watched as the older woman wrote a few notes on the papers the Dean had left her. When Missus Pittsfield placed them on the right hand corner of her desk, Carol recognized the motion as the signal for her to get her own coat on. By the time Carol had retrieved her coat from the hook on the back of her door and had shrugged her way into it, Missus Pittsfield was standing at the door, her coat hanging from her frail shoulders, her purse clutched tightly under her right arm. Carol stopped at her desk to turn off her computer screen and watched the name "Ramone Cortes" fade to black. Maybe, Carol thought, she was beginning to care whether her boy toys had a name. Too dangerous, she admonished herself, better not to know—or care.

5

THE DAY AFTER THE BIA BOARD MEETING, BEN MET
Marc Lipoff at a donut shop in Newtonville. The sound of cars
racing along the turnpike into and out of Boston penetrated the walls
of the coffee shop and became a roar whenever the shop door opened.

"Ben, I could describe the villages and proposed development sites
to you, but I think it would be a lot easier to visualize if we took a ride."

"Works for me."

After coffee and a donut, Ben and Lipoff climbed into the waiting
Suburban and drove along both sides of the highway, down to Newton
Corner, back into Newtonville, out to West Newton, Auburndale and
Newton Lower Falls. Only the latter village avoided the long surgical
scar of the highway, but it sat across the circumferential road, Route
128, from the rest of Newton. The compactness of the village centers
and the character of the residential neighborhoods abutting them impressed Ben. He was less impressed by the poor attempt to knit together the Newton Corner village with a large concrete complex of offices,
hotel and garage. The complex didn't make the highway crossing any
more comfortable and it created a high wall between the two halves of
the community.

The design possibilities energized Ben. Each village would need
a unique solution. He told Lipoff he would take on the project and
asked how much it would cost to acquire the land and the air rights to
proceed.

"I think we're a long way from buying land," Lipoff said. "We need to develop a design that can be presented to the mayor, the aldermen and the community. Newton can be a tough place to get anything done."

"But surely a design that knits the villages back together would be seen as positive."

"It's hard to believe anyone would prefer the status quo of the moat that is the turnpike, but there will be those who do."

"A moat protects. This scar just offends. We will create a design that returns a vibrant village life to these places."

Lipoff reached out and took Ben's hand, shaking it vigorously and clamping his left hand around Ben's forearm. "Let's get started, Ben."

6

I N THE QUIET OF THE PROFESSIONAL OFFICES, MO
Sather's deep, angry voice rattled the walls.

Shouting from the conference room was becoming a more frequent occurrence—as well as an incentive for Cheryl to start looking for another job. She liked working in the same building as her husband, but the fighting amongst the partners at Campbell, Brown and Sather stressed her so much that she was having trouble sleeping.

It actually wasn't much of a shouting match. The shouting came solely from Morris Owen Sather. Walter Brown had a whiny plaintive voice, and when he spoke, Sather seemed to become more belligerent. Arthur Campbell tried to act as the mediator, but he, too, felt the blunt force of Sather's bullying.

HALF AN HOUR after the meeting began, two men dressed in nearly identical black suits and buttoned up white shirts with narrow collars and no ties entered the office and approached Cheryl's desk. Cheryl braced herself to greet them and inform them as kindly as she could that the firm didn't allow religious solicitation on the premises. One of the men—the shorter of the two—asked for Mister Sather, but didn't look at Cheryl. His eyes darted around the room, seemingly looking for something, but failing to find it. The taller, more robustly built man stood silently, his arms slightly bent, his hands resting near his coat pockets, his eyes on Cheryl.

"Mister Sather is in a meeting right now."

"He'll see us," the taller man said—not as a command, but as an explanation.

"He's expecting us," the smaller man said, somewhat apologetically.

Cheryl rang the conference room phone. "There are two gentlemen here to see Mister Sather."

A short pause.

"I'll ask," Cheryl said into the phone. She looked at the shorter man. "Could I tell him your name?"

"We have a package," he said.

"They have a delivery for Mister Sather." Cheryl nervously gnawed on the end of a ball-point stick pen.

Moments later, the door opened and Sather appeared, yelling back into the conference room, "Don't you go any where. This isn't over."

He approached the taller man, who pulled an envelope out from under his jacket. The man offered it to Sather who took it, nodded, then turned and walked down the corridor towards his office. Cheryl watched him until he was out of sight. She then turned to address the two men, but they were gone. She half-thought about looking under the furniture and in the coat closet for the taller one, but just then the phone rang.

SATHER CLOSED THE door to his office and locked it. He walked to his desk and took a silver letter opener from his top drawer. He was about to slice the top of the envelope open when a loud commotion coming from the direction of the reception area caught his attention. He dropped the envelope on his desk and headed for the door. Screams punctuated the commotion and Sather broke into a trot, finding a crowd at the doorway to the conference room.

Pushing through the bodies, he yelled at the people to go back to work. He emerged from the crowd into a large room. At the far end, he found Walter Brown laid out on the floor, motionless, his right hand clasped to his left arm.

"Cheryl, call an ambulance," Sather yelled.

Cheryl cupped her palm over the receiver to call back to Sather, "They're on their way."

Sather slammed his palm against the conference table. He kicked a chair so hard that it hit the wall, scattering papers that had been left on its seat. "Dammit," he said. "This is inconvenient."

Cheryl wondered if he knew he'd said that aloud.

WHEN RAMONE GOT off the elevator and entered the reception area, Cheryl was waiting for him.

"Sorry, Ramone," she said. "I have another job for you. There's an envelope in Mister Sather's office with the approved submittals for the bank project. It must be delivered to the contractor, MacAfee, by the end of the day. Get it and deliver it."

"But I have a class at the BIA in forty-five minutes," Ramone protested.

"So you'll be a little late. Go get it and leave now." Cheryl watched Ramone shuffle down the corridor. She had to remind herself that she was married and very much in love with her husband. Still, Ramone was a very pleasant eyeful.

RAMONE WALKED INTO Sather's office and found the gray envelope on his otherwise empty desk. It struck him that Sather's office always looked as if no one worked there. At least, he thought, he didn't have to go rummaging through piles like he'd had to in poor Mister Brown's office.

He was headed down the corridor when the EMT's emerged from the conference room with Mister Brown on a gurney. They stopped in the corridor to adjust the oxygen mask on his face and to make adjustments to a bag hanging from a rod near his head. The large crowd in the reception area compounded the time the EMT's took in the corridor and it took almost fifteen minutes for Ramone to get to the elevator lobby. He avoided the elevators and bounded down the fire stairs two steps at a time.

"Damn them," he thought. No one at MacAfee would need the envelope tonight. He would go to class and deliver the envelope before they opened in the morning. He could slip it under the door like he had done a few times before.

"CHERYL!" SATHER YELLED as he entered the reception area just as Cheryl was taking her purse out of the bottom drawer of the desk, preparing to go home. "Who has been in my office?"

"No one, Mister Sather," Cheryl pleaded. "Wait. Ramone went in there to get the package that you wanted him to deliver to MacAfee. Why?"

"Nincompoops! All of you. Where is he now?"

"He left to deliver the package, then go to school."

"He didn't take the package for MacAfee. He took..." Sather stopped mid-sentence, waving the MacAfee envelope wildly above his head. He slapped it on Cheryl's desk. "Never mind."

Anxious to have MacAfee return the envelope without seeing its contents, he stalked back to his office. Frantically, he called the MacAfee office and learned that Ramone had not shown up.

Sather assumed that the kid had probably opened it and knew what he had. Worse yet, he might actually be an FBI plant. Who knew anything about the kid? He worried about what he had to do next, about the fallout, about Dashkov's reaction. He picked up the phone and dialed. "Vassie, it's Mo. We have a situation."

7

R AMONE CORTES HAD THE LOOK AND BEARING OF A
fighter—short-cropped, curly black hair and an olive complexion, broad biceps fronting well-defined triceps, a strong neck that grew
from well-muscled shoulders and steady dark eyes that gave away little
but seemed alert to any movements around him. He wore the black
beret many of the BIA students wore. Tonight he wore the red T-shirt
that Carol LaPierre had given him on their second date, with black
slacks and Chuck Taylors with no socks.

When Ramone left the BIA that night, he walked the four blocks
to Copley Station, dodging groups of four to six young people—mostly
students—who stretched across the width of the Newbury Street sidewalk. He enjoyed the attention of the eyes that followed him, especially
the eyes that engaged his own before looking away. He counted the
pairs of eyes he thought he could have if he wanted. The number had
climbed to twenty-two by the time he reached the Copley Station head
house.

Ramone boarded the E line trolley. Finding the car nearly empty,
he headed toward the rear of the car. He stumbled and lurched as the
train started up, nearly falling backward into the last seat.

At each of the next half-dozen stops, a few people boarded the trolley and then got off it two or three stops later. None came further back
in the car than the middle door. By the time the trolley left Brigham
Circle, the car had become empty again, except for one old man who sat

immediately behind the driver and two men who talked sports—mostly about the prospects for another Red Sox collapse.

At Fenwood Road, six or seven young men boarded, all wearing red T-shirts and red bandanas. They immediately walked to the rear of the car and began talking loudly—"but not belligerently," as the driver and the old man would later state in their interviews with police investigators. The young men all got off the trolley at the Back of the Hill stop, leaving behind the one guy in the black beret they would later recall. At Heath Street—the last stop after the MBTA converted the line beyond that point to buses—the driver approached Ramone, who stared right at him, slouched back in his seat.

"Hey, buddy," he said. "Last stop. You have to get off."

When Ramone didn't answer—did not move, did not blink—the driver knew he was dead.

8

CLAUDINE LEANED ON THE DRESSER, HOPING FOR THE nausea to pass, but the blackness still enveloped her. She struggled to stand. In a few moments, the nausea passed and the light returned. She realized that something was very wrong. She had been able to dismiss the continuing headaches and the back pain as stress. The vision problems she blamed on too much time staring at a computer screen. She thought she might have blacked out while sitting on a bench when she was waiting for Emma's dance class to end, but maybe she had simply dozed off.

Claudine had never liked—nor trusted—doctors. She hadn't seen one since Emma was born seven years ago. She treated any ailments with either diet or neglect. Her only medicine was a daily dose of vitamin D.

It was time, she knew, to call Isabel Deschamps. Perhaps tomorrow.

"MISTER MAYOR, THIS is Ben Holt, who I told you about." Lipoff drew his arm around Ben and ushered him towards the Mayor. "As you know, I have been working with Ben and his firm to develop plans for the development of air-rights over the turnpike. He has brought some drawings for you to see."

The mayor stepped forward and offered his hand, jamming it into Ben's and shaking heartily. "Great to meet you, Ben. May I call you Ben? I've asked some folks to join us. This is my chief aid, Jim Britton, and this is our City Engineer, Jimmy Mullane. Our planning director, Jim Barry, will be joining us. See, I never have to go to the gym, they come to me." He laughed heartily at his own joke.

Ben thought that a gym might, in fact, do the mayor some good. He was very short, with a stout neck and deep chest. His legs were stubby and thick—like piano legs—and extended from an ample belly to tiny feet. The entire package was clad in a custom dark gray suit that sought to hide its contents, with only moderate success.

Ben had already checked out the mayor and knew that his outgoing, almost corny, personality belied his sharp mind. He had been an alderman, a successful businessman and a state legislator. He was demanding and had high expectations of everyone around him. They loved him for it.

After the planning director arrived, Ben rolled out his plans and proceeded to describe the projects he envisioned. Two of the villages, West Newton and Auburndale, would have new landscaping and sound-controls walls built along the roadway, but no new large-scale development. Some of the under-used one story properties in each village could be developed with two- or three-story buildings, maybe an occasional five-story structure, but Ben's firm would not be involved in those projects. The Newton Lower Falls village would remain untouched, except for the redevelopment of a chemical company site that lay along the Charles River. Ben's group would not be involved in that, either.

Ben turned over a large sheet of paper and revealed the projects for Newton Corner and Newtonville that he thought would interest Satart Holt and its development partners. Newtonville would see two large residential developments, one on each side of Walnut Street, which crossed the turnpike at a right angle. They would have retail at street level and would connect to the existing railroad station below. The height of the buildings would be five to seven stories and none would be taller that the steeple of the adjacent church and a Mason's Hall beyond. The façade along the Walnut Street bridge would be set back to allow for outside dining. A one-story parking garage would be sandwiched between the retail story and the residential floors above.

The Newton Corner development would be more complex. It would include a new railroad station, a three-story shopping arcade, and office buildings arranged so that the tallest structure sat at the L-shaped intersection of the existing hotel and the office structure. The heights of the office structures would descend to a level of four stories as it approached the neighborhood. In order to connect the new complex across the ring road that surrounded the site, new housing developments of five to seven stories would be built on parcels north and south of the ring road and would be connected to the central development by bridges that housed small neighborhood shops on either side.

"This is wonderful!" the mayor exclaimed. "I wish you luck and hope that you are successful. My people are at your disposal." He spoke just as the planning director walked in and silently mouthed "sorry" toward his boss. The mayor stared at the late arrival who noisily pulled out a chair from the far end of the table and sat, fiddling with a pad of paper and patting his chest looking for a pen in his jacket pocket.

"Great. Then we have your support." Ben smiled at the mayor.

"Oh, I won't take any official position on this. I have no legal standing on land use matters. You will need to deal with the aldermen. But I'll be following your progress and I wish you luck."

The mayor stood. All of his staff stood with him. They filed out of the mayor's office, followed, after another hearty handshake, by Ben and Lipoff.

"What did we go through that for?" Ben asked.

"He can't approve our project, but, if he's not on board he can kill it by ordering neglect."

"Interesting. Where do we go now?"

"We meet with the local aldermen, one by one, and then we gird ourselves for the neighborhood meetings."

9

"**I** 'M GOING TO MISS YOU, LIZ." ANNIE WRAPPED HER arms around her daughter's neck and pulled her close. She was a few inches taller than Annie now. Her kinky red hair was gathered in a pony-tail and Annie recalled when she had to redo Liz's pony-tails when she was a child. Liz could never seem to get it quite centered on the back of her head and she was particular about its symmetry.

"I'm only going to be in New York, Mom. It's not like we're moving to East Oshkosh."

"No, but East Oshkosh is safer."

"Mom, Brooklyn is perfectly safe." Liz wasn't sure that she believed that, but that was the party line. Besides, Kevin was a big, strong guy.

"Well, I still don't like it a whole lot."

"I know, but it's a great opportunity for Kevin, and I already have interviews set up with three companies."

Annie pushed her chair back from the table and got up with her cup in hand. She reached for Liz's cup. "More?"

"Just one, then I have to go. Kevin and I are interviewing photographers today. I hope that we find someone good. We waited too long. The wedding is only six weeks away."

"Ah, my baby, marrying a kind and handsome man, just like in the fairy tales."

"Yes, I finally got me a killer man who is not a killer."

"Liz! You know that I hate that talk."

29

DIANE SAT ON the second step of the stairs of the East Brookline Street brownstone where she and her husband had just purchased a condominium on the third floor of a four-floor walk-up. She was waiting for Josh to arrive with the rented truck and their furniture. She had arranged three folding beach chairs across two parking spaces to reserve space for the truck and the ramp that would slide out from the truck's back. She wished she had borrowed lawn chairs from Annie; they were taller and looked much less foolish than the low-slung beach chairs.

As she sat she ran her fingers through her bobbed blacked hair. She took a folding mirror from her bag and checked the roots above her forehead for any sign of gray. She smiled when she was satisfied that, despite missing her hair-coloring appointment last week, all was well.

Diane was about to beep Josh when she saw the truck round the corner at the far end of the block. He was driving slowly, probably looking for a parking space. Diane jumped up from her seat and ran into the road, waving her arms over her head. It took a few moments for Josh to notice her. When he did, he smiled his toothy smile at her and waved. She thought of how much she loved him.

CAROL SAT IN front of the television, half-watching Jay Leno, more than a little surprised that Ramone hadn't called. She intended to tell him she wasn't going to be seeing him anymore, but she wanted him to call her. Finally, getting more annoyed that he hadn't called yet, she picked up the phone and dialed his number.

"Hello. Ramone here. You know what to do."

After the beep, she thought for several seconds about what she might say, then pushed the button to end the call.

WHEN THEY HAD finished unloading the truck with the help of a half-dozen friends and a lot of pizza and beer, Diane and Josh decided to take a late evening walk around their new neighborhood. The heat of the day had receded and a sea breeze arose, adding a slight chill. Josh took the sweatshirt that had been lying loosely tied on Diane's shoulders and held it open for Diane to wriggle in to.

They walked down to Albany Street, the up to East Concord and passed the building where Josh was about to start his research fellowship, working on a new and promising cancer treatment. They stopped and considered the building for a few moments—rather non-descript for such important work, Diane thought—then continued down to Washington Street, crossing through a small park and back to East Brookline Street and home.

Diane had hoped they would make love for the first time in their new home that night, but when she emerged from the bathroom freshly showered, she found Josh sound asleep.

10

ANGEL PISCARA LIVED IN LEXINGTON, MASSACHU-
setts in a 1960's development known as Five Fields. It was the
second land development in the same Lexington neighborhood execut-
ed by The Architects Collaborative. Many of the homes were owned by
architects and designers—some of whom worked at TAC. Hideo Sasaki
lived near Piscara, as did Jared Whiting, who ran the Satart Holt office
in Boston.

Ben had stayed with Jared and his wife Marisol, while his penthouse was being added to one of the buildings at Ocean Park. Ben's
apartment atop the Satart Holt offices in the Back Bay had been an-
nexed to create more space for the growing firm. Ben hadn't liked Five
Fields much, but he appreciated now the opportunity it gave him to
spend more time with Piscara. Every time he gave Piscara a ride home
he remembered how much he disliked the development.

BEN BROKE THE long silence that accompanied his ride with Piscara from the Back Bay. "What did you think of the meeting tonight?
Sather was up to his usual form."

"Sather is a profoundly evil man."

Ben turned to look at Piscara for an instant and saw that the old
man's eyes were closed and he was facing straight ahead. Ben couldn't

recall Piscara ever having said anything directly negative about anyone. He didn't seem to dislike anyone for the same trivial reasons everyone else all too frequently did. If Piscara judged someone to possess a character flaw serious enough to deserve his enmity, he would simply ignore him or her. To not exist in Piscara's eyes was the greatest damnation he could offer.

Ben continued. "I spoke to Sather and Theroux, Dean. I made it clear to them that they are not authorized to have any discussions with other colleges about their potential interest in acquiring the BIA unless the Board has fully discussed the matter and approved even preliminary discussions. They claimed they had not done so, although I know that they did, and I know who they met, when and where. I didn't tell them what I know, and Sather silenced Theroux before he could ramble on in his usual way and reveal more than he should. Theroux outsmarts himself sometimes, trying to construct an excuse for his actions. I assume that Sather asked for the executive session tonight to discuss the potential for a merger with one of the larger schools. At least two of them in the city have talked about starting an architecture school, as has one of the suburban schools. It's getting a little crazy. We've got four architecture schools in Boston now and two more in Rhode Island. I don't see how the market would support one more, let alone three, and I don't see how a merger would benefit the BIA. But I don't think we can sit back and do nothing. I want to expand the school—probably add an interior design school and a landscape architecture school. Tell me what you think."

Ben paused his soliloquy, waiting for a response from Piscara. The light from an approaching car illuminated Piscara's face. His eyes were closed and his face immobile. Ben turned his attention back to the road, glancing occasionally in his rear view mirror, looking for the reassuring headlights of the black Suburban.

Twenty minutes later, Ben pulled to the side of the road. No sooner had he stopped when Piscara pulled on the door handle.

"Don't you ever get tired of them following you?" Piscara said, without looking at Ben.

"Sometimes, but…"

"Goodnight, Holt." Piscara stepped out of the car. As he started to close the door, he stuck his head back in. "Make room for an artisan program in your plans, as well," he said. He closed the door and waved to the vehicle that had been following them—his standard wave, a half raising of his left arm. The black Suburban pulled sharply to the left and blocked the road for Piscara to cross. The man in the passenger seat jumped from the truck and used the beam of his flashlight to light the roadway in front of Piscara. Ben watched as Piscara walked down the dark drive to his house, entered the pool of light by his front door, and disappeared inside.

THE NEXT DAY, Ben and Marc Lipoff met eight aldermen—six individually and two together. It was to be seven, but one of the aldermen had brought a colleague. Four of the aldermen were enthusiastically in favor of Ben's proposals, two claimed interest but wanted to get feedback from the community, one was adamantly opposed and one was silent. The alderman who was opposed served as chair of the Land Use committee of the aldermen and lived across town from the development. He worked as a city planner in another city. The silent alderman was the president of the board and a land use attorney. Ben had thought that these two would understand and appreciate his proposal more readily than the others. He was wrong and unhappy about it.

"It doesn't mean that they will both vote against us," Lipoff said. "Okay, so Manchester definitely will, but that's only one out of twenty-four."

11

CLAUDINE MADE AN APPOINTMENT TO SEE ISABEL
Deschamps for late in the afternoon, when the doctor would be
finished with all of her other patients. Two days before the appointment
she had her assistant, Genevieve, cancel. A minor crisis involving the
late delivery of some handwork from an Italian *passamenterie* supplier
provided the excuse.

Isabel called Claudine's atelier that evening after her office hours
were done for the day, and offered to come see Claudine at home.

"She's really busy getting ready for Fashion Week," Genevieve explained. "I doubt she'll reschedule until after she returns from the hol-
iday she takes after the shows end."

"She has made three appointments since January and has canceled
them all."

"I know." Genevieve cupped her hand over the phone and whispered, "Her headaches seem to be getting worse. We're all quite worried, you know."

Isabel asked, "Do you know if Ben is in town?"

"He travels three days a week, but he's in Paris Friday through
Monday."

"Thank you, Genevieve. Don't worry, it's probably just stress."

ISABEL CHECKED HER Rolodex for Ben's telephone number. She was happy to see that she had his cellphone number as well as his office and home numbers. She decided to call him late Saturday morning to invite him and Claudine to dinner. She knew that Claudine would be at work by then and she could make plans with Ben directly.

AS THE JET reached cruising altitude, Ben withdrew a gridded computation notebook from his bag. He opened the book across his lap and started sketching diagrams populated with circles, rectangles and squares—with an occasional triangle—all connected by either solid, dashed or dotted lines. This was the seventh such diagram in his notebook and it stretched over two large pages.

Satart Holt had come through the recession that ended the 1980s in great shape. The success of the Ocean Park project brought new commissions for waterfront development in St. Petersburg, Florida, as well as in San Diego and Philadelphia. A developer had recently met with Ben about the redevelopment of a former military base on an island off San Francisco, and there were the potential projects in Newton.

The Paris office was working on studies for the redevelopment of the Hotel Miramion, which sat on a site along the Seine facing Notre Dame and the Ile Saint-Louis. I was a historic seventy-five-room mansion that had been relegated to use as a warehouse for the Paris hospital system. The work in Yemen had been cancelled, but a large new waterfront development in Montpellier was on the boards, as well as a few small museum projects that had grown out of Ben's design for the Gallerie Satart.

There were dozens of other smaller projects, too. The Satart Holt firm now had European offices in Paris, Milan, Berlin and London; U.S. offices in Boston, New York, Miami, San Diego, San Francisco, Philadelphia, Chicago and Washington DC, as well as Pascal's office in Rio and an office in Shanghai.

Though Ben still owned 61 percent of the firms stock, and Jared and Paul each owned 5 percent, there were twenty-two other shareholders among the principals—mostly studio directors.

A FEW WEEKS earlier, Ben had been sitting at a table on the patio at Bart and Yeti's in Vail when a young man at the next table had noticed Ben's Satart Holt baseball cap and introduced himself. He worked at the SHA office in San Diego and wondered what Ben's connection to the firm might be.

It was at that moment Ben decided it was time for a change.

12

ISABEL CALLED JUST AFTER NINE ON SATURDAY MORN-
ing.

Ben was sitting under the arbor, pondering whether to refill his coffee cup that had grown cold. His computation book sat open up-side-down on his lap and fell to the ground when he reached for his cell phone. *"Bonjour."*

"Bonjour, Ben. It is Isabel Deschamps."

"Hello, Isabel. I'm sorry, but Claudine just left for her atelier. You reached me on my cell."

"I did want to speak with you, Ben, and invite you and Claudine to cocktails tonight."

"We'll be at the ballet at Chaillot tonight. I'm sorry."

"Yes, we'll be there too. If you can't stop by before, we'll see you there. A *bientot."*

"Au revoir, Isabel. A *bientot."*

ISABEL CALLED HER friend, Georges, the producer of the ballet and arranged to get two tickets for that evening.

13

A T EXACTLY NOON, BEN CLOSED HIS NOTEBOOKS. HE loved sitting in the garden, writing and sketching, but work and the BIA conspired to deprive him of the time he wanted to spend there.

The doors from the house opened and Emma emerged and ran to him, leaping into his arms almost before he could open them to catch her.

"Da-dee, are you ready? Daniel is ready and Pascha is looking for his shoes."

"Yes, Emma, I am ready, but I can't go."

"Da-dee, it is Saturday."

"Yes, but I haven't had my morning kiss."

"Oh, Da-dee." Emma wrapped her arms around him, kissed both cheeks and gave him a sweet, soft peck on his lips. "Now you have been kissed, Da-dee."

"Let's go then."

EMMA AND BEN walked into the house and found Daniel in the foyer leaning against the front entry door, his arms folded across his chest.

"Pascha, time to go," Ben called up the stairs.

"I can't find my new sneakers," came the response.

"Look in your laundry basket." Ben looked to Daniel who answered with a wry smile and shook his head.

A moment passed and Pascha called out, "No."

Ben tried again. "On your bookshelves, under S."

Daniel nodded.

A few more moments passed.

"Found them," came the call from upstairs.

Pascha never seemed to realize that it was Daniel who was playing tricks on him, or that tricks were being played on him at all. Pascha was a brilliant child, but the concept of someone playing a trick on him eluded him. For Daniel, torturing Pascha was his own, private form of entertainment.

THE SMALL TROUPE headed off through Saint-Germain de Pris on their way to lunch and to Luxembourg Gardens with a detour or two along the way. Gunter and one of his men followed in the black Suburban—discreetly, but never out of sight.

WHILE THEY WERE standing in front of the window of the umbrella maker, Daniel spoke. "Ben, I'm going to be leaving the firm this summer."

Ben's lips curled in a quirky smile. He had expected this and was satisfied to know that his intuition was good. "I'm sorry you'll be going, Daniel, but not surprised. What are your plans? Have you told Claudine?"

"No, you're the first to know. Fifth—actually. Simone and I are going together. To Brazil first to see Pascal and Severine. Perhaps to stay with them for a month or two, then to Australia and South Africa, then back by way of Central America."

"Are you...?"

"Getting married. No. Probably not, anyway."

"No, not that, though it wouldn't disappoint us if you did. Are you looking for your grandmere?"

"Yes."

Ben pondered the face of his son and took in the full measure of the man he had become. He had expected this day—expected to fear it, but he did not.

"I will keep your secret until you tell Claudine. Do not make me wait too long."

"Yes, sir."

Ben wrapped his arms around Daniel, drawing him in. Daniel was a full two inches taller than Ben now, but would always be his child. The child of his love for Claudine. He was the child Ben had learned to be a father on. As they drew apart, they each reached to wipe something from an eye—a bit of sand perhaps.

14

NEARLY TWO AND A HALF DECADES AFTER MEETING
Claudine, Ben could still be struck by her beauty and the wave
of reaction she caused in any crowd, large or small. Strangers in a bis-
tro would engage her in immediate and intimate conversation, and
she seemed to hear more of what they said than Ben ever did. The
strange thing, in Ben's mind at least, was that he was more forgiving
of the trivial inanities that Claudine despised. He was, he thought, the
more approachable one, while Claudine was more aloof. When he asked
Claudine about the apparent anomaly, she would simply answer with a
Gallic shrug. They had arrived at Chaillot and the rear passenger doors
opened simultaneously when they came to a stop. The red carpet ran
from the curb, up the stairs to the front door. Gunter held Ben's door.

"Thank you, Gunter," Ben said.

"IT'S NICE TO see the two of you," Isabel smiled, her right arm
wrapped in her husband Bernard's left.

"Are you tracking me down because I've cancelled so many appointments with you, or are you here for the ballet?"

Isabel froze.

Bernard spoke up, saving Isabel. "Now there is an idea, Isabel.
Maybe you could partner with Claudine to develop a line of tracking

devices hidden in a necklace, like the beautiful **VCA** that you're wearing. Maybe it could contain a hidden stethoscope. We could make millions."

It took a moment for Isabel to recover and smile at Bernard's joke. In the meantime, a server appeared between her and Claudine.

"May I offer some Champagne?"

"Isabel took the proffered glass from the silver tray, as did Bernard, but Claudine declined. Ben would have liked some—his mouth was a bit dry—but he declined, as well.

"Claudine, I need to visit the boy's room before the ballet starts."

"I think I will too," Bernard said, and the two men headed off.

For a few moments the two women were silent, looking uncomfortably around the room at other patrons.

"Can I talk to you for a moment, Isabel?"

"Of course."

Claudine led Isabel to a small alcove off of the lobby. She told Isabel about her fainting spells, her headaches and her nausea. Isabel held two fingers on Claudine's wrist as she looked at her watch. She raised Claudine's eyelids with her fingers, first left, then right. She asked Claudine to open her mouth and stick out her tongue. She looked at Claudine's gums. "You need to come into the office so that I can do more."

"What are you thinking?"

"Well, for one thing," she said. "You're pregnant."

15

B EN PICKED UP THE RINGING PHONE. "HELLO."
"Mister Holt, this is Emily Pittsfield, the Dean's secretary."

"Yes, Missus Pittsfield?"

"The Dean would like to see you at your earliest convenience. Tuesday at five p.m. would be fine."

"I could see him on Wednesday, same time, Missus Pittsfield."

"I'm sure that will be fine."

The line went dead. Emily Pittsfield, like the Dean, somehow suffered from a greeting deficit—no "hello" and no "goodbye." Ben was sure that Missus Pittsfield had caught the disease from the Dean. He wondered where the Dean had picked it up. He had met Piscara's family and knew his brother quite well. If anything, they exhibited an overabundance of greetings. It often took a flood of hellos and kisses to start any interaction with them—even in business meetings—and the goodbyes could stretch on for half the night. Ben wondered whether Piscara's occupation as a sculptor was a factor; stone didn't require hellos or goodbyes.

As Ben was writing the appointment in his notebook, he realized he had not even thought to ask what the meeting was about. He realized that the Dean was only one of three people who had been able to schedule a meeting with him without an agenda revealed. The other two had been Claudine and Pascal.

He picked up the phone to call Pascal, then set the receiver in the cradle. It would be only six o'clock in the morning in Rio and Pascal had never been an early riser.

WHEN BEN ARRIVED at Dean Piscara's office that Wednesday, Carol LaPierre was about to leave for the day. She had her coat almost on and her lipstick had been recently freshened. Ben recalled the young man with a bouquet of flowers he has passed in the lobby.

"Ah, Mister Holt," she said. "Are you here for a meeting?"

Missus Pittsfield interrupted, "Please come in, Mister Holt. The Dean is ready for you."

Ben smiled an apology at Carol. "Yes, apparently I am."

As he and Carol turned sideways to slip by each other through the doorway, Ben noticed the moist gleam in Carol's eyes and thought that, as much as he loved Claudine, he liked the occasional affirmation that he got from attractive women. Carol was indeed an attractive woman. She was in her early fifties, but passable for ten years younger, trim and scarcely wrinkled. Her hair was always impeccably blonde and her lipstick unmistakably pink.

BEN SAW THE familiar form sitting in one of the two chairs in front of Piscara's desk, but it took him a moment to realize who it was. He called out, "Bill Button."

Button turned in his chair, then rose to face Ben. He hesitated for a noticeable moment, but offered his hand.

Ben looked at the hand for a noticeable moment, then raised his own and reached for Button's right arm, pulling him close and embracing him. "How are you? How is Amélie?"

"We're both well. She misses her mother, probably now more than ever, but we're well and she still loves her father. So we're well."

Ben nodded.

Piscara said, "I was unaware that the two of you knew each other."

"Yes," Ben said, "we've shared some adventures."

It was Piscara's turn to nod—one slow expressive nod of his head with his massive eyebrows accentuating the movement.

Piscara said, "Button has quite the tale to tell. If it's true, we have another of your adventures on our hands."

16

ON TUESDAY, BEN HAD ARRANGEMENTS MADE FOR him to fly to Rio the next week. He was surprised to hear that Claudine had asked to come along as well. He had assumed that she would still be busy making preparations to fill orders from the Paris Haute Couture show that had ended only five weeks earlier.

Ben had thought it would be nice to spend some time alone with Claudine, but she wanted to bring the children to spend some time with Oncle Pascal and Severine. Daniel wanted to bring Simone so that the two of them could survey the Rio scene in preparation for their sojourn. Gunter wanted to bring his team, as well, but Ben suggested they try to limit the size of the team. In the end, Gunter brought nine—including himself—from a team of twelve. And Claudine's insistence that Robert and Babette come along to visit some of their ex-patriot Italian family in Brazil swelled the party to seventeen, not counting the three staff members in charge of coordinating the travel arrangements and Ben's two assistants, Jacqui from the Boston office and Segolene from the Paris office, who'd somehow gotten themselves attached to the crew.

Gunter had two of the black Suburbans flown to Rio ahead of their plane. The Suburbans would arrive two hours before the rest of the entourage, who would then be ferried to their Rio quarters in the two armored vehicles, as well as in another one, which Gunter had acquired for them in Brazil.

When the president of one of the big American furniture manufacturers, Herman Miller, heard of the trip and the size of Ben's travelling troupe, he offered the company's 707—complete with crew—to Ben, who was happy not to have to deal with commercial flights and airport security. He had expected to travel to see Pascal alone and had ended up with an army.

When they arrived at the airport in Brazil they were met by a Delgado—chief—from the DPF, the Brazilian Federal Police, who was an old friend and college classmate of Gunter. He told Gunter that the Holt group would have to wait in the airport's VIP reception area for a short time while a high-profile traveller from Colombia cleared the arrivals area. Through the huge glass windows overlooking the tarmac, Ben saw a short, elegantly dressed man surrounded by eight or more large men clad in jungle fatigues, wearing black berets and toting black AK-47's.

"Carlos Y," Gunter said. "Either hero or villain, depending on what side you're on."

"What side is he on?" Ben asked.

"Friend to the peasants, benefactor to the arts, assassinator of rivals. The latter is only rumor, of course, but rivals do tend to disappear."

"I wonder what brings him here."

"I'll ask." Gunter walked over to his friend, who was busy flirting with Claudine, spoke to him for a moment, nodded and returned to Ben.

"You're not going to believe this. He was here to meet with Monsieur Satart."

AFTER A WAIT of just over twenty minutes, the Holt entourage was on its way, the black Suburbans with two police motorcycles in front and an un-marked Brazilian Federal Police car with lights pulsing, following.

As soon as the entourage pulled through the gate in the tall, solid wall that surrounded Pascal's gardens, all of the garden workers stopped working and stared at the three black Suburbans. Severine emerged from the house and stood, smiling, in the entry portico as the second Suburban pulled to a stop in front of her. Ben exited on the far side, but Claudine emerged on the right and was immediately embraced by Severine.

"Claudine, I am so happy." Severine spoke and smiled simultaneously. "I have heard the marvelous news."

"Thank you so much, Severine. I am looking forward to spending much time with you while we are here. I'm sure that we'll see very little of Pascal and Ben."

Severine took Claudine's arm. "Come, let's go into the house. You must be tired."

Pascal came around the corner from the back of the house riding a small tractor. Ben was struck by how much Pascal had taken on the look of an old French farmer. He was wearing old brown overalls and a blue chambray workshirt. "Ho! You are here! It has been so long that I wondered if I would recognize you. You are a wonderful sight for these old eyes."

Ben beckoned to his three children. They took turns hugging Pascal and kissing his cheeks three times.

Daniel presented Simone who kissed Pascal on both cheeks.

"Ah, I am only a *bisou bisou*, eh, my dear?" Pascal said. "Perhaps by the time you leave I will be promoted to three."

Simone blushed and Pascal took her hand and led her into the house, followed by the rest of the family.

BEN AND PASCAL sat on the edge of a stone watering trough that had been converted to use as a reflecting pool in a private garden behind the house and adjacent to Pascal's studio.

"So, Ben, what brings you here?"

"Can't I just come to see my great friend?"

"Yes, of course you can, but I sense that you didn't".

"Yes…no, not entirely, but I did want to come to see you. I have been wanting to for a while, but there was always some reason why I couldn't. In fact, that's why I did." The two men looked into each other's eyes and renewed an old connection.

"You know, I've wondered when you would, if you would. I know that I don't come up for board meetings any more, probably for the same reason you are here. What are you going to do?"

Ben described the growth of Satart Holt. As he listed the chronology of events that had occurred since Pascal had moved to Brazil, Pascal nodded at each: openings of new offices; several offices with fifty or more staff members; increasingly large new projects including three new extremely tall buildings—and Ben disliked very tall buildings; expanding services that Ben felt diluted the firm's purpose; a management committee that soared past thirty members and was closing in on forty; and nearly thirty million dollars in annual revenue.

When he finished with the litany, Ben talked about the steps he had taken to better manage the firm: limiting his direct reports to six—although that had recently grown to seven; decentralizing management of the several offices while maintaining central financial control; creating studios within the firm so that talented designers could flourish. "All of these steps have worked well," he said. "Although some of the studios needed adjustments, mostly the replacements of studio heads who were great designers but poor managers or poor humans."

Pascal responded, "That is to be expected."

"I suppose, but I didn't."

"So what has changed your mind about your direction? It all seems quite brilliant."

Ben said, "I think that I have become Marcel. I love him and admire him—now more than ever—but I never wanted to be him".

"So?"

Ben continued. "I think that the germ was planted while I was in Vail, sitting on the patio at Bart and Yeti's, eating a burger with snow banks all around me—yet my face still hot in the mountain sun."

"That sounds nice enough to change anyone's mind. So you've decided to become a ski instructor and give up architecture?"

"Almost. While I was eating, I set my Satart Holt cap on the table. A guy and his girlfriend came and sat at the table next to me and the girlfriend pointed out my cap."

"Ah, great marketing." Pascal exclaimed, his arms shooting into the air above his head.

"It turned out he works for us in San Diego. So he started talking about the firm and its work. He's proud that he works for Satart Holt and his girlfriend agrees."

"Very good."

"Then he asked a question that floored me. He wanted to know who I was and what my connection to Satart Holt was."

Pascal laughed, "No. Was he surprised when you told him?"

"I told him that I *used* to work there."

Pascal fell back in his chair and grabbed the edge of the table to steady himself. "Why?"

"I didn't want to embarrass him in front of his girlfriend."

"That was very kind."

"It turns out that I want to make it true—almost."

Ben described his plan for selling off most of the firm. Some of the smaller offices he wanted to sell intact, say the San Diego office as an example. Some of the larger ones he would like to split up. New York might be split into two or three offices with up to three studios each. There would be a transition period—hopefully no longer than eighteen to twenty-four months. Satart Holt would slim down to four offices: Paris, Boston, a smaller New York office, and Rio.

"You don't need to keep Rio, you know. I won't go on forever, and Severine would understand. Don't do it for us."

Ben responded, "I'm doing it for us—you and me; mostly me. It is still Satart Holt."

"It is interesting though. While everyone else is building ever larger firms with acquisitions, you are looking to grow smaller."

"I like that idea—grow smaller."

"When will you announce this?"

"Soon after we return. I'd like you there beside me."

"I will be there."

Ben changed direction. "Good, that's done. The next thing on my plate is more difficult. Bill Button visited with Angel Piscara and me recently and had a story to tell that makes some sense and could be a blockbuster if it checks out. It may involve your friend, Mister Y."

"He's not a friend. He's a cold-blooded killer who is using real estate to launder his drug proceeds. He came to me offering a project—a jewel, in fact. I turned him down. Who did he kill this time?"

"No one that I'm aware of. He has had people asking about his son who came to the U. S. under an assumed name. The son and his father were estranged, most likely over the father's business. They think that he may have come to Boston. He wanted to study architecture so they have been checking for him at the BIA and the Cambridge schools. That was just one of Bill's stories and I would have forgotten it except that I saw Mister Y when we arrived."

"What is Bill up to these days?"

"You never really know with Bill. He still has some connection to the Feds, but I'm not sure whether he works for them or is some kind of independent operator."

"He had another story?"

"I need to check out a few things first. I plan to have Doug Strout look into it. Bill has a habit of concocting stories that suit his agenda. I should know more soon."

17

EARLY THE NEXT MORNING, BEN CALLED DOUG
Strout. Doug had been his investigator and a valuable source after
his brother Don's death. Strout had provided the identity of Don's killers and the hood who put the contract out on him. Ben had wanted to
even the score for Don, but someone else had made the hit first. Making
the call to Doug unleashed a torrent of memories, good and bad. He
hadn't thought of Don for a while, but speaking with Doug reminded
Ben how much he missed him.

Ben laid out his conversation with Bill in outline form, using ro-
man numerals for major points and cascading through alphanumeric
designations for questions and queries that might support or refute his
assumptions. In twenty minutes he had laid out the case for Strout,
ending in point IX: Carlos Y.

"Now there's an enigma." Strout whistled, as if to emphasize his
statement.

"Why is that?"

"He has led quite the varied life—or lives. Hard to believe they're
all the same guy."

Ben said, "I've heard the cold-blooded killer part."

"Actually, that was a well-concocted story, but never true, at least
not directly."

"How so?"

"He was a farmer and part-time accountant for an American fruit company when he was recruited by our side. He was young and ambitious and turned the opportunity into his first fortune. Then we switched sides and had no further use for him. Our new friends attacked his farms and burned him out. He barely escaped into the countryside and found new friends, raising an army and financing it in part with his own fortune, supplemented with drug proceeds from his new friends and smart investments."

"Smart investments?" Ben asked.

"Yes, indeed. In fact, the gasoline that fueled his enemies' vehicles and helicopters was supplied by one of his companies."

"How in hell did he pull that off?"

"The true ownership of the company was hidden behind a shell based in Bermuda," Strout explained.

"Bernadine?"

"One and the same."

"So, why is he free now, flying to Rio to try to engage Satart Holt?"

Strout said, "The Reconciliation Court set him free. He's now a businessman and philanthropist. He has achieved a rather impressive record on the second count: funding loans and grants for small farmers; providing drugs to fight diseases in Central America and Africa; working among rock stars, actresses and business tycoons."

"Sounds like a saint."

"Don't turn your back on him," Strout admonished.

18

AFTER BREAKFAST, BEN AND CLAUDINE EXCUSED themselves and announced their intention to take a walk around Pascal and Severine's property, making the point that they intended to walk alone.

Claudine was forty-six and would be forty-seven by the time the baby, Abeille, would be born. She had expected this to be a difficult pregnancy given her age, but to this point it had been surprisingly easy with the exception of some light-headedness and occasional near-blackouts. She half-reported her symptoms to Isabel, but failed to be truthful about their severity or their frequency. This would be her last pregnancy and she didn't want any interference.

AT FIRST VIEWING, Pascal's house seemed to be a copy of the Villa Savoye, but a more careful viewing revealed a number of differences. The garage had been banished to a separate structure on a spur drive beyond the house; the columns—or *pilotis* were slightly more substantial and the planning grid was five by five, not the four-and-a-half that the Savoye had been reduced to; there was a third floor that was set back from the main floor and aligned vertically with the ground floor; and the glass on the north and east sides ran floor to ceiling making the building's interior far more open to the surrounding land.

The house and its outbuildings—the garage, studio building, four-suite guest pavilion, a paddock and stable and a residence for the live-in staff with attached utility storage and a wood shop—sat on two and a half acres of heavily wooded land adjacent to a large city park. The proximity of the Parque Natural Municipal Penhasco Dois Irmaos made the property seem even larger than its unusually large size for the Leblon suburb.

"I AM VERY happy for Pascal. He has found Severine and this wonderful place."

"Yes," Ben said. "He seems so happy and full of peace here. I miss him though. I miss sitting at the café table with him, saying nothing or saying everything."

"I could sit at the café table with you."

"Hah!" Ben said. "For all of ten minutes, then you'd run off with another dress design in your head."

"Perhaps."

"I'd love it though—sitting with you, saying nothing and yet everything."

"So you still love me?"

"Not still. There's nothing still about it." Ben looked deeply into Claudine's eyes.

Claudine swept a stray lock of hair from Ben's forehead. "So when are you going to find the time to spend those ten minutes with me?"

"Soon. Before Abeille is born. I'm working on a plan to split off and sell most of the firm."

"Is that why we're here?" Claudine asked.

"Yes."

"Have you told Pascal yet?"

"I have. He said that it is my decision to make since I own the majority of the firm." Ben described to Claudine the plan he had shared with Pascal, including the plans to keep the four offices.

"Have you made a final decision?"

"Yes. When we return, I'll meet with all of the shareholders. Once I do, the news will leak out quickly so I'll have to be prepared for an expedited implementation. Perhaps we'll make a public announcement within seven to ten days after the details are worked out. It'll be a brutally demanding schedule, but it will be over soon."

Claudine reached out and softly rubbed the back of Ben's hand. "Is it hard for you? Hard to let go? You've built an impressive firm."

"No. It has been too hard to hold on. I've become a manager of manager's managers. That's not what attracted me all those years ago."

"And you want to be Pascal."

Ben smiled. He hadn't thought about it that way. "And I want to be Pascal. I want to smell pencil shavings and the way that dust smells when you turn on your drafting lamp and burn it. I want to rub rubber cement from my fingers. I want to wash pencil lead dirt from my hands or smudge it across yellow trace. I don't do that anymore."

Claudine laid her head against Ben's shoulder. "Hold me."

19

EARLY THE NEXT MORNING, PASCAL SUGGESTED THAT Severine take Ben on a tour of the work that she was doing in Rio. Ben readily agreed and they planned to meet at eleven.

"I think that you will find her work refreshing, Ben. You and I take the credit, but she has a fresh voice and a wonderful eye."

Severine was ready at eleven with a printed itinerary of the projects they would visit: three private homes, two large housing developments, two office buildings and the headquarters of an NGO that provided free health care to migrant workers.

Gunter drove the Suburban. Segolene sat in the passenger seat beside him, a large backpack with cameras and lenses crowding her legs. In the third seat sat two men in black t-shirts, matching pants and dark glasses with AK-47's across their laps.

Their first three stops were at the private homes. They were all one story in height with low-slung roofs and broad soffits. Two had thick masonry walls covered in stucco, the third was clad in a highly-figured cream-colored marble called Crema Bâltico that had been quarried near the owners' birthplace. Large walls of doors opened onto terraces surrounded by lush greenery. Other than the doors, there were few glass openings.

Ben was impressed by the quiet peace of these places. The design was restrained: no tricks, nothing to call out for attention. Severine commented that the darkness of their interiors was part of the reason the houses stayed cool without air-conditioning. Ben noted that the houses were warm in the middle of the day, but not hot.

All three homes were nice, Ben decided, but he loved the light. He would have to stay in Paris.

Their next stop was at the site of the two office buildings, nearby each other in a park-like setting. Severine told Ben that she had wanted to try to building these buildings without air-conditioning as well, but the corporate parents of the two companies that occupied them—both US oil companies based in Texas—were wary of attracting executives to an office building without refrigerated air. If she had missed the opportunity to bring fresh air into the buildings, she had not missed the opportunity for creating a fresh, exciting design. One of the buildings was clad in brightly colored metal panels, the glazing of its windows held in equally bright steel frames. The effect in the Brazilian sun was brilliant, both literally and figuratively. The dark greens of the park setting set off the bold colors and the three-story building shone like a jewel. Ben thought it was one of the most appealing, refreshing office designs he had ever seen. He felt proud that Severine was a part of Satart Holt.

The second office building was almost as colorful, but in a more subdued way. It had about a quarter less glass and its wall faces were covered above and below a ribbon of windows by a colored ceramic rainscreen. The effect was more subdued than the first building, though more textural. Ben found the two designs equally impressive and thought that he'd be hard-pressed to pick a favorite.

The offices of the NGO were part of the same park as these two buildings, but they were accessed by a separate drive off the main street that served the park. It turned out to occupy—thematically and visually—a separate world, as well. It was more low-slung than the first two offices, being only two stories high, with the second story rising from the broad low-sloped roof of the first story and capped by its own shallow-sloped roof, though with less a broad overhang. Its walls were of rough granite, which set off the finely finished mahogany window frames. The roof was constructed of a gray-green anodized standing seam aluminum and Ben immediately recognized that Severine had probably wanted to use copper but that the aluminum had been a concession to cost.

No sooner had the thought formed, when Severine confirmed it. "It wasn't even the cost," she said. "It was the perception of the cost." The building gave the impression of being a river-side pavilion in the forest and, though it was of a different vocabulary than the first two, it was clear that they had all been created by the same hand. "There is a connection between the work they do here and the two housing developments we will see next, and it is not a pleasant one. You will see when we get to the site, but I wanted to warn you."

Ben wondered why she felt the need to warn him, but he decided to wait until they got to the site to raise any of his questions.

THE HOUSING SITES, two adjacent sites owned by two different developers, both Federal agencies, were huge and barren. The few living things apparent from the approaching drive were wind-beaten trees that looked like they were well on the way to being dead. The site consisted of two low hills with what appeared to be roads winding between them. As robotic-looking machines moved around and over the hills, they kicked up clouds of dust that swirled skyward until they were caught by upper-level breezes and forced back down towards the ground in rotating cones that reminded Ben of widow's peaks. The housing consisted of five eleven-story buildings on the two sites, partially surrounded by five-story elements that radiated from the towers in a four-vaned windmill pattern. Like one of the office buildings, the towers and low elements were clad in colored terracotta panels, but, unlike the linear texture of the office buildings, these panels were more sculptural, reminding Ben of some of the concrete block patterns in Wright's buildings. The window frames were the same brightly colored hue of one of the office buildings, but the character of the color told Ben that these were anodized aluminum. The building begged to be liked, and Ben felt torn by his own desire to like them and the inhumanity of the scale of the development. He wondered if Severine felt the same.

Ben turned to Severine and said, "I think you did a great job with a difficult project. The scale is haunting, but the buildings are pleasant and well thought out. Why the warning?"

"Wait until we reach the crest of the first hill."

As they approached the crest, the reason for Severine's warning became clear. In the ravine that rimmed the site on two sides sat a favela of ramshackle shelters—barely more than tents—that stretched several hundred meters until the land rose again. "Are these the people that the housing is being built for?" Ben said.

"No, they are the shacks of the construction workers and their families. When this project is done they will leave, taking little with them, and move on to the next favela at the next construction site."

Ben sat silently. He was profoundly saddened by what he saw, but could find no words.

Finally Severine spoke. "I want to cry when I see this. I want to stop designing housing like this, but it does good for a lot of people. It provides a living for the workers and their families, but there is no opportunity for escape for most of them. Their children will do the same as they do and they will take care of their parents as their parents now take care of their own parents. The NGO tries to help, but the problem is so big and the solutions so expensive. The only people getting rich are the developers and the government agents."

"And us," Ben noted aloud.

"Yes, and us."

"Can we give the money back?"

"To the government? That would be foolish. We support the NGO, but they don't have the capacity to use as much as we'd like to give them. As bad as this is, it is a developing country and there is no easy first-world solution. We pick at the problems but we don't solve them."

"Let's plan to try. At least we have to do that." Ben took the notebook from his pocket and scribbled a note.

"We can talk."

"Can we visit the camps?"

"You don't want to do that." The voice came from the seat behind Ben.

Ben looked into the rear-view mirror to catch Gunter's eye. Gunter shook his head.

They rode back to the house in silence.

20

B EN CALLED THE PARIS OFFICE AND SPOKE TO ERMA, A
secretary there. "I gave most of your messages to the others as you
asked, but there were three that said that they had to talk to you. They
weren't on your list of calls to be referred."

"Okay. Who?"

"Mister Strout said that he had some answers for you, but he'd have
more by tomorrow if you wanted to wait. A Mister Carlos E called. He
said that he'd like to see you while you were in Rio. Oh, and he said
that he spelled his last name with a Y, but I'm not sure what he means."

"That's okay, I do. He spells his last name Y," Ben explained.

"No, I'm sure that he said that it's E."

"I'll explain later."

"Okay," Erma said tentatively.

"And?"

"Oh, yes, and Isabel Deschamps called."

"That one is for Claudine."

"No. She made the point that she wanted to talk to you."

"Hmmm. Odd. I'll call her now."

"That's it."

"Thanks, Erma, I'll call tomorrow."

BEN CALLED THE number that Carlos Y had left and was somewhat surprised when Y answered the phone himself. They made plans to meet for a late lunch the next day at a café on Ipanema Beach.

THE CALL TO Isabel Deschamps took a little longer to put through with Ben being shuttled through three operators before finally being connected to the doctor.

"Thank you for calling me back, Ben," Isabel said when the call finally reached her.

"Not a problem. What can I do for you?"

"Is Claudine with you? I mean, in the room with you?"

"No, she's in the garden with Severine."

"I'm sorry. I know I shouldn't be talking with you, but I need your help."

"Okay?"

"I need to see Claudine. I've called her repeatedly but she doesn't return my calls. It's quite important."

"Is it about Abeille? About the baby?" Ben asked.

"No, not at all. It's about her. I'm afraid that's all I can tell you."

"Well, I can try, but unless I know more it will be hard for me to do anything more than ask her to contact you and I don't think that will go very well."

There was a long pause while the doctor considered her options. Ben could hear the public address calls in the background. He imagined that she was wrestling with both sides of her obligation to her patient.

"This is not how you should learn about her illness, I'm afraid," Isabel finally said.

"Probably not, but that's not important right now, is it?"

"You know about her fainting spells, no?"

Ben said, "In general. She tends to downplay them."

"I don't understand 'downplay'."

"Minimize their significance."

"Yes."

"So, are you telling me that there is something more serious than overwork and the effects of pregnancy involved?" Ben asked anxiously.

"We think so, yes."

"So you don't know."

"I'm sorry, Ben. In substance, we really do know a fair amount. I am very sorry. Claudine has a growth on her brain. There is an eight in ten chance that it is not benign."

Ben slumped back against the wall, felt his knees give way, and slid to the floor.

"Ben?"

Ben could hear the blood rushing in his ears and felt a pause in the beating of his heart.

"Ben, are you still there?"

Ben found that he couldn't speak. He tried but he choked before the words would form.

"Ben? Ben?"

Ben swallowed hard. "Yes...I'm here...Isabel, are you telling me that Claudine has brain cancer?"

"We think so, yes."

"Damn it. I don't want to hear that you think so. Does Claudine have brain cancer?", Ben demanded.

"It's extremely likely, yes."

Somehow Ben found the strength to put himself into rational mode. He and Isabel talked about the likely prognosis, the probable progress of Claudine's illness, the possible treatments —very few for her form of brain cancer according to Isabel—and the probable effects on Claudine's pregnancy of both the illness and potential treatments that Isabel wanted to try.

"You know she won't agree to anything that will jeopardize the baby," Ben said.

"We don't want to wait longer than necessary to start treatment, and her delivery date is almost three months away."

"Is there a treatment that wouldn't imperil the pregnancy?"

"There is one, but it is very experimental and has only been tested in lab animals."

"Tell me about it."

"I am not an expert on this. I have read that they use a focused beam of radiation and a robot of some kind."

"Can I talk to them? Are they in Paris?"

"No. They are in Boston. Ben, it's a very small company that grew out of research at Boston University Medical Center. I don't think that it's good to get your hopes up."

"Doctor, it seems to me that hope is all we have. I want to talk to them. Can you make that happen?"

"I will call you tomorrow morning. Can I have your cell phone number so that I don't need to go through your office?"

"Yes, of course." Ben gave her his number. She asked for the prefix for Brazil and Ben explained that she would just need to dial the prefix for France.

"Thank you, Isabel. Please trust me. I will do anything for Claudine, but I will do nothing foolish."

BEN FELT HOPEFUL about the Boston connection immediately after the call, but moments later, reality punched him in the solar plexus and he struggled to breathe. He realized that he had never, ever fought a battle this big. For the first time in years he was truly scared. The enormity made him feel weak. Denial, he knew, was the first stage of grief. He had to harness denial for his own purposes, to make it his strength.

His most immediate need was to be with Claudine—to talk with her, to hold her—but he wasn't sure that he could. He rose from the arm of the chair on which he had been sitting and walked from the house. He headed down the hill toward the ocean, feeling an urgent need to walk in the tides. As he walked, the colors around him seemed unrealistically vivid and the sounds around him loud and sharp, but he saw nothing and heard nothing. They were just colors and noise. He had to get to the sea.

It was almost dark when he realized where he was. He had left his shoes somewhere and the cuffs of his linen pants were wet with seawater. His pocket was tingling and when he reached to rub the spot he realized that his cellphone was ringing. He pulled the phone from his pocket, flipped it open and saw "Gunter" on the tiny screen. He raised the phone to his ear.

"Gunter, please pick me up at the beach. I'll be walking back toward you."

WHEN HE GOT back to Pascal's, everyone had gone to bed. He went to his bedroom and found that Claudine was sitting up in bed, waiting for his return.

"Are you still comfortable with your decision about the firm, Ben?"

"Yes, Claudine, why do you ask?"

"I know that you like to walk to think. Is that why you went to the beach alone?"

"To think? Yes, to think and to gather strength for all that lies ahead. Thank you for understanding me so well, Claudine. I love you."

"And I love you. You see, it is futile to try to keep secrets from me."

"I would never try." Ben lied to Claudine for the first time since they'd met so many years before. It would not be his last.

21

UNABLE TO SLEEP THAT NIGHT, BEN QUIETLY SLIPPED from their bed and went out to the patio to sit in the moonlight. A battle lay ahead and the prospect of it made him nearly euphoric— much as would the prospect of starting a major new project—but as soon as the high feelings peaked, a door would slam inside him and he would sink into a black despair.

As the light began to break through the strands of clouds against the horizon, Ben rose from his chair, went back to their bedroom and slipped into bed against Claudine. He nuzzled her shoulder, breathing her in, and fell asleep.

"MISTER HOLT, I am honored to meet you." Carlos Y was not a tall man, but he had heft and a commanding presence born in a lifetime of leading men in battle, whether in war or in business.

"Thank you. I am most intrigued to meet you, Mister Y," Ben said, offering his hand.

Y took Ben's hand and shook it with a slightly too firm handshake. "Please, you must call me Carlos."

"Carlos, then."

There was a momentary silence between the two men, then Carlos Y smiled and motioned Ben towards a seat just inside the café. Four large men—black-clad even in the Rio heat—took seats at two empty tables along the sidewalk. Two tables remained empty between the four men and Ben's table. The half of the café along the far inside wall was crowded, but no one sat in the half of the room between Carlos and the small bar.

"You fit well Pascal's description of you."

"I will take that as a compliment," Ben said.

"Perhaps. We shall see."

"I know that you have been talking to Pascal about some work that you would like us to take on. Pascal speaks for the firm. Why did you want to speak to me?"

"It is not about work that you might do for me. It is about family, about my son."

A waiter approached and stood quietly beside the table.

"Ah, Paolo, good morning. I will have my usual," Y said, without looking up.

"Good morning, sir. Yes, sir, and for your guest?" The waiter turned to Ben.

"Two eggs, chorizo, a small bowl of salsa. And a glass of last night's white wine."

Carlos nodded toward the waiter who shuffled off toward a window in the wall at the far end of the bar.

"You were saying, about your son?"

"Yes. Carlos is my youngest and most difficult child. The only boy in a sea of girls. We have not been very close for some time, Carlos and I. I have not spoken with him in almost three years. He was away at school, then when he graduated, he moved away within the week. Now he appears to be missing."

"How would you know?"

Carlos' face turned dark, but was quickly lit by a smile. "He is very close to his mother and to my wife, Marcia. He spoke to each of them weekly until several weeks ago. They are very worried and very unhappy."

"And you?"

"Unhappy women do not make life pleasant."

"What do you think, and why do you think I can help you?" Ben asked.

"I think that he wants to live his own life, to live on his own terms. I admit that it is unlike him not to call his mother or Marcia, but this may be part of the separation that he wants. Marcia showed me some of the boy's sketchbooks. I never knew of them. They are quite good. Almost all of them are of buildings he liked. One was of a museum you designed to hold Pascal's work."

"So that is how you found us."

"No. Marcia went to school with Severine in France. It was a bad time then and we sent our children away to school. Marcia and Severine became close friends."

"Ah."

"So I am thinking that Carlos might want to be an architect. You are an architect who runs a school, no?"

"Not quite. I am the chair of the Board of Trustees but, believe me, I do not run the school."

"Perhaps, but you can make inquiries."

"Yes, but where. There are an awful lot of architecture schools in the United States and you don't actually know that he is in the United States."

Carlos reached into his jacket, removed his wallet, and withdrew a photograph. He handed it to Ben.

"Red sox cap. Okay, maybe, just maybe, he is in Boston," Ben said, grimacing. "I'll see what I can find out. Can I take this?"

"Yes, of course."

"I'll check around, but he could be anywhere, and not necessarily in architecture school."

A car backfired down the street and the four men on the sidewalk stood and massed shoulder-to-shoulder between Carlos and the street. When they realized the source of the noise, they relaxed and sat down again.

Carlos smiled. "Rio can be a dangerous place. You should have security."

A waiter approached with their food. It was a very different waiter than Paolo who had taken their order. Carlos looked up at this new waiter, surprise and a glimpse of fear in his eyes.

"Thank you, Gunter," Ben said.

Gunter nodded to Ben and walked away.

Carlos smiled again. "Yes. You fit well Pascal's description of you."

AFTER BEN LEFT, Carlos reached into the inside breast pocket of his cream linen jacket—crisp, even in the Rio humidity—and withdrew a small, worn picture of a boy, perhaps thirteen. He set it on the table and smoothed it out with his fingers, working from the center into the corners. He raised his glass to his lips and took a small sip, his eyes never leaving the photograph. "Be safe, my son."

22

B EN CALLED ISABEL DESCHAMPS FROM THE SITTING
room in the main house in Pascal's compound. "Isabel, I have a
favor to ask of you and I hope that you can accommodate me."

"Yes, Ben?"

"I want you to keep our earlier conversation a secret. Can you do
that?"

"Perhaps. It was I who initiated a clearly unethical, probably un-
lawful, conversation. I was speaking as a friend, of course—not as a
doctor."

"So there is no reason to reveal it."

"I may have some misgivings about that at a later date, Ben, but
for now, no. It will remain between us."

"I will do my best to steer her into a reasonable treatment protocol.
I have a friend who is an investor in health-related start-ups. I plan to
ask for his help."

"There are accepted protocols for her disease now, but I have to
admit they are primarily palliative. I was hoping you might do something to help her. I have nothing much to offer her."

"Isabel, it is highly unlikely that Claudine would take drugs that
might affect Abeille."

"Abeille?"

"The baby."

"You've named the baby?"

"Claudine did."

"Of course."

BEN SAT ON the edge of their bed and watched Claudine as she briskly brushed her short hair at the dresser opposite the French doors. "Claudine, I need to go to Boston this week. Just for a day, maybe one night. Will you come with me?"

"If you promise to take me to New York when you are done. I need half a day there."

"Will you be alright with so much flying?"

"I think so."

"Then we will go. We'll go alone. No need to decamp everyone."

"Ben, can we talk about something?"

A lump rose in Ben's throat and his "Yes" came out high-pitched and hoarse.

"Are you okay?" Claudine asked, reaching out for Ben's arm.

"Yes, just swallowed the wrong way. Of course we can talk."

"I want to deliver Abeille in Boston."

"Not in Paris?"

"No." Claudine lowered her gaze to the floor between them.

"Okay, I guess. It's your choice. Is there anything wrong?"

"No, but I'm older and if there are complications, Boston is the place I'd want to be. They have some of the best specialists for both Abeille and I. I may be silly, but why take the chance."

"I agree—about the specialists, not that you are silly."

"Then it is settled."

"It is settled."

NO SOONER HAD Claudine left the room when Ben took his phone from his pocket and flipped it open. He dialed the number that he had found on his Palm Pilot.

"Hell-oh."

"Gene, It's Ben Holt. I *will* be able to come see you this week. Probably Wednesday if that works for you."

"Anytime after ten is fine, just let me know. That's my report reading day so I'll be happy to have the interruption."

"Great, I'll confirm Wednesday by tomorrow."

BEN MADE SEVERAL more calls: one to arrange to have the Learjet flown to Rio to pick up Claudine and him on Tuesday evening; another to Doug Strout whose voicemail always made Ben smile—"no names, no messages, please"—and a call to Carol LaPierre to see if the young Carlos Y might be a student there. She told him she didn't think so, but promised to check the records.

23

"IT'S GOOD TO SEE YOU, BEN. HOW LONG HAS IT BEEN? Two years?" The two men were seated in winged armchairs in the Parker House dining room. It was a restaurant Gene often used to meet executives from health care and pharmaceutical companies that were seeking an investment from Gene and his venture capital firm.

"About that, I guess. How are you, Gene, and how is Joan?"

"Very well. Very, very well. Our youngest just got engaged and we're about to have our second grandchild. Everyone is healthy and happy. What more can we ask?"

"That's pretty much it, I'd think," Ben said.

"How about you? The family well? How is Marcel? He doesn't come to board meetings anymore."

"Marcel is getting by, and getting on, of course. His physical health is good for a man his age, but he is very lonely."

"I've seen the pictures of the parties on his boat. It seems like he's trying to out-Hefner Hefner." Gene laughed a small, short laugh.

"Yes, well, you can be surrounded by people and still be lonely. He has never stopped loving Bernadine." Ben stroked his lips with the forefinger of his right hand.

"No offense, but he may be the only one."

"Perhaps."

The waiter approached and took their drink orders. Ben asked Gene if he was ready to order lunch.

"You go ahead. I'll be ready by the time you're done."

"I'll have the quiche, salad and a side of fries. And the fries must be very hot."

"Yes, sir."

"Health food, Ben?"

"Gotta keep my duck fat levels up."

Gene ordered and the waiter bowed slightly before leaving.

"So you're interested in targeted beam cancer therapies. An investment?"

"Yes, I'd be willing to invest, but it has to be in late stage trials or better."

"Are you ill?"

"No, not at all, but please don't dig any deeper than that. I'd have to betray a confidence and that would be a problem."

"Marcel?"

"Gene!" Ben's back stiffened and his hands tensed visibly.

"Okay, okay." Gene raised his palms toward Ben.

"Do you have anything?"

"There are some opportunities. I've listed them here." Gene withdrew a single, tri-folded sheet of paper from his jacket pocket. "I left off the chemo work because they're not targeted and not beam technology, although there is some early, interesting work on targeting of chemo therapies. And I left off the gene therapies because it's much too early in their development to consider them unless you are looking for a high-risk investment with dubious likelihood of a return. That leaves three groups developing various forms of radiation therapy delivery. Two of the groups are here in Boston; one is in Cleveland. Marcel actually has a substantial investment in the Cleveland group."

"Who is the farthest along?"

"Probably the Boston University Medical Center group, but the Cleveland group is better funded."

"Hmmm." Ben rubbed the side of his forefinger across his lips, his thumb anchored under his chin.

"I can see the Holt brain churning."

"Do you have an investment in the BU group?"

"My team controls the management, although BU owns the intellectual property rights to the research. If you tried to buy them out you'd be tied up in review committees for years while they try to figure out how your generous offer is part of some hidden agenda. The more you offer, the more they'll worry."

"I know John quite well."

"Silber? He could make it happen with a wave of his good hand. There would be a huge outcry, of course, but he wouldn't care, but he would take a healthy slice of your profits down the road."

"Well, it's a bit early for that. Can you arrange a meeting with their lead researcher?"

"I can and will. Give me a week or two."

"Okay. No longer though."

"By the way, I forgot to ask—how are Claudine and the baby?"

'The baby is doing well."

Gene searched Ben's eyes and found what he was looking for. "Good luck, Ben," he said.

24

A FTER LUNCH WITH GENE, BEN HEADED TO THE BIA
to keep an appointment with Angelo Piscara. He stopped at Carol
Lapierre's office first and stuck his head through the open doorway.

"Any luck with Mister Carlos Y?"

"Good afternoon. No, nothing. He hasn't been a student here.
I was thinking though that I could check the other local schools. It
would be easier than you having to go through channels." Carol shifted
her weight from her left leg to her right, smiled at Ben and arched her
neatly-trimmed eyebrows.

"That would be great, thanks."

"Do you happen to have a photo?"

"Yes, I do. I need to get copied, but I'll get it to you. Thanks again
for following up on this."

"No problem."

FOR BEN, ONE of the downsides of visiting Piscara at the BIA was
that he would likely run into George Theroux, whom he had come to
dislike intensely. George was a smart guy with a big ego but for some
unknown reason he allowed himself to be controlled by Mo Sather. The
oddity was that the more Theroux strived to mollify Sather, the less
respect Sather had for him.

Ben had watched Sather bully Theroux relentlessly. Ben wanted to feel bad for Theroux—perhaps even to protect him—but a series of incidents proved that Theroux was less than trustworthy.

Ben realized that it was just a matter of time before he would have to act to remove Theroux. Today, however, Theroux was away at a conference and Ben was spared from having to see him.

"GOOD AFTERNOON, MISSUS Pittsfield, is the Dean ready to see me?" Ben had approached the Dean's secretary's desk unnoticed.

"Oh, yes. Yes, but may I speak with you first?" Missus Pittsfield looked straight at Ben's face, something he had never seen her do before. He realized for the first time that her eyes were a striking blue-gray.

"Of course."

Missus Pittsfield drew a piece of paper from her top desk drawer and handed it to Ben. There were three columns of names, single-spaced.

"The Dean noticed that there has been a surprising surge in membership applications in the past month. Almost one hundred and twenty new members have paid their dues in the past two weeks alone. He asked me about this and I did some checking, but I haven't yet told him what I found."

"And that was?"

"Nine of them were from current or former students, many of whom paid in cash."

"Okay?"

"Sixty four of them were paid with one check."

"From?" Ben asked.

"Campbell, Brown and Sather."

"Interesting. And the others?"

"Mostly twenty or so memberships paid with single checks from other large firms."

"Can you put together a list of these for me?"

"I already have." She handed Ben two more sheets of paper w:th copied images of three checks on each.

He folded the sheets in half, blank side out. "Will you announce me now?"

Missus Pittsfield walked into Dean Piscara's office, stopping just inside the door. Ben noticed that she held onto the doorknob, resting her weight on it. The Dean and Missus Pittsfield had grown old together and it was hard to think of one without thinking of the other.

"Mister Holt is here, Dean."

Ben barely heard Piscara's hoarse, bearish voice come from deep inside his office "Holt. Yes. Send him in."

THE BIA WAS unusual among colleges in many ways—open enrollment, mandated work/study, an all-adjunct faculty and low tuition—but most unusual was the accessibility of its governance. For nearly a century, one could become a voting member for ten dollars a year. Ben had led an effort to raise the fee to fifty dollars, but it remained at ten dollars. Every member had an equal vote in electing officers and directors and approving by-law changes. The college accrediting board railed against the BIA's egalitarian approach and called it unstable, though it had clearly worked for more than a century.

"HOLT, IS THERE any news about Button's allegations? Have you been able to confirm them?" Piscara said.

"Not entirely. We have confirmed that Campbell, Brown and Sather are working with a developer on a large plot of land adjacent to the BIA that has been assembled over the last ten years or so and held in the names of several owners that we—we being Doug Strout, my investigator—have identified as straws."

"Are you sure?"

"It was hard at first since all of the owners had different addresses, but Doug decided to visit some of the addresses and found the common link."

"And that was?"

"They were all Mailbox, Et Cetera locations. Doug had one of his younger operatives—a rather fetching young lady—sign up for a box there and have Victoria's Secret send her packages. It was almost too easy. The rather portly, middle-aged manager was soon in full swoon and he never blinked at giving her the names and forwarding addresses of the boxes she inquired about. I believe that he wanted her to see how important he was."

"Hmmm." Piscara didn't even smile, but then Piscara never smiled. "And the forwarding address was?"

"The offices of Campbell, Brown and Sather."

"That's rather significant, no?"

"That's rather significant, yes."

"I wouldn't think that they'd have that kind of money. Would you?"

"It's unlikely that they do. We're still working that angle."

"So what can we do with what you have?"

"Substantially nothing. CBS apparently controls a large piece of land adjacent to the BIA. Big deal, nothing illegal there. Sather is pushing his plan to have the BIA merge with BU. Maybe he's just a visionary. It's all background for now, but it's good that we know this and he doesn't know that we know."

"Good, good. Now you'll drive me home."

"Of course."

AS BEN DROVE towards Lexington, Piscara closed his eyes and snored lightly. As they were crossing the Sozio Circle rotary towards Common Street and the Belmont line, Piscara spoke without opening his eyes.

"Holt, what are you going to do about Sather and the other large firms loading the voting membership with their own people?"

"I don't know yet. How much do you know?"

"The Architectural Association of Boston board discussed it and urged other large firms to participate. There is likely to be more large firm memberships coming. You won't see that in the minutes, if you intend to check. I only heard because Fitzwilliams is still a friend of the BIA."

"Can I talk to him?"

"Yes, he's expecting your call."

Piscara sat quietly for a few minutes, then resumed his snoring, stopping—as usual—only a few blocks from his home.

As Ben pulled up in front of Piscara's house, he noticed the familiar headlight of a vehicle that pulled to a stop a few hundred feet behind him. It was a comfort knowing that Gunter was there, but why hadn't he pulled across the road to block any traffic as was his normal tactic? Then Ben remembered that Gunter wasn't with him tonight, he was with Claudine. Piscara was half way out of the car before Ben's attention returned to the Dean.

"Good night, Holt."

He was gone before Ben could respond. He crossed the road and walked down the drive to his house. Ben waited until the entry light went out, then pulled onto the roadway and drove away slowly, his eyes on the lights behind him. When he had driven a hundred feet or so the lights followed. He lost them for a moment when he rounded a curve and worried that they may have stopped at Piscara's house, but they soon reappeared and followed him until he reached the highway.

When he turned left after the bridge onto 128 South, he noticed the lights turn onto 128 North. He decided that his "tail" was probably just a coincidence, but a discomfort remained in his gut.

25

THE MORNING BROKE CRISP AND BREEZY, BEN'S FA-
vorite kind of day. He had one meeting set up for the morning,
then he and Claudine would be heading to New York.

JOSH HANLEY WAS a tall, thin handsome man with thin blue eyes
and a moppish head of thick blonde hair, making him look like a California surfer, which, indeed he had once been. He looked to be in his
late twenties, although Gene's notes indicated that he was approaching
fifty. He had been an accomplished and adored epidemiology researcher
before becoming interested in targeted radiation therapy for hard to
treat cancers. While his demeanor was personally modest and unassum-
ing, his passion for his work was infectious and people loved working
for him, notwithstanding the long hours and relatively low pay they
all endured. Josh had a way of talking about the treatment protocols
as if they were live, sentient beings. Ben found the dichotomy between
Josh's personal demeanor and his price for his team and their treatment
protocols utterly charming.

The team had developed three treatments in various stages of late
animal trials—one each for cancer of the liver, pancreas and brain. They
were just beginning trials on a promising prostate cancer treatment.

Ben was filled with hope that he had found the treatment he needed for Claudine despite Josh's oft-spoken cautions about future outcomes in the on-going tests. As they were parting after the meeting, Josh wondered aloud whether someone like Ben's father-in-law might be interested in making a gift to support their research. He also mentioned that they were trying to raise money for new facilities.

"I'm sure that you understand the importance of a well-designed and constructed facility to support our work." Josh said, looking at Ben's forehead, avoiding direct eye contact.

Ben found it a bit odd that this smart, accomplished scientist who was on the verge of producing brilliant, life-saving technology also had to be a common shill.

Ben promised to raise the question of a gift with Marcel.

AS SOON AS the Learjet lifted from the runway, Ben laid his book, open-side down, on his lap and watched Claudine's face, her nostrils gently flaring as she breathed deeply, her eyes closed, her lips pursing slowly as she exhaled. She was as beautiful, he thought, as she had ever been, but her beauty belied the ugly disease within.

"I want to talk about how we are going to treat your cancer."

Her eyes opened wide and Ben could feel the anger in her stare, but he thought he saw a glimpse of fear as well.

"Have you been talking to Isabel Deschamps behind my back?"

Ben decided that it was time to confront Claudine about her illness. "This isn't about Isabel Deschamps. Did you think that I could not see the signs? The fainting, the loss of balance, the confusion?"

"You don't know that my pregnancy doesn't explain all of those."

"Claudine, I am not a fool and this is not our first pregnancy. This is different."

"No, you are not a fool."

"So, let's talk."

"I will not agree to any treatment until after Abeille is born and weaned."

"I will agree to no treatment until after Abeille is born. Period."

Claudine narrowed her eyes and stared at Ben. She saw that he returned her determination with his own. "Promise?"

"An absolute promise."

"You won't let them try?"

"There is no 'them' to try anything."

"You hear stories."

"Ah, but none of those stories are about us."

"I think that I'm glad you now know."

"Tell me everything."

Claudine did, and her words broke Ben's heart.

"I MET A man today who could change the course of my research—if he wants to." Josh sat at the table across from Diane, picking at his dinner.

"Really, who is that?"

"A guy named Ben Holt who is..."

"An architect, married to a French fashion designer and whose father-in-law is an insanely wealthy manufacturer? Yes, he could."

"People Magazine?"

"No. He was Annie's high school boyfriend. We spent a lot of time together back then."

"Hmmm. Interesting. Gene sent him to see me."

"Is he interested?" Diane asked.

"Yes, I think so, but I got the feeling that it's more than a gift he's considering. I think he wants to make an investment."

"That wouldn't be surprising, especially if the money came from the father-in-law; although I suspect that Ben and Claudine make bundles on their own."

"No, not just a money investment. Something closer to home. It was the way he pressed me on efficacy. Not approvals, efficacy."

26

IT WAS AN ODD REQUEST, BUT CHERYL HAD COME TO
expect odd requests from Mo Sather. She was to stay late on Thursday
evening to help set up for a meeting with a special client. When the
client arrived, a call would be made from a limousine outside the building and Cheryl would promptly leave her desk and walk to the back
fire stairs, taking them to street level and leaving the building by way
of the back alley.

When she asked the name of the visitor, she was told that she didn't
need that information.

At five minutes before seven, the call came. Cheryl rang Sather's
office and informed him that his visitor was coming up, then she left as
instructed and walked the ten flights of stairs to the back alley. There
she met the night guard who had been told to wait for a call from the
same limo, then wait in the back alley until someone from Sather's
office came to get him.

The guard lifted the brim of his guard's hat, one that reminded the
guard of his enlisted serviceman's hat, which is why he wore it. The
security company had changed to ball caps a decade or more earlier.
"Good evening, ma'am." He quickly removed his hat and placed it
under his left arm.

"Did you get the call, too? The voice was definitely Russian. I
fought with Russians in W-W-Two. I know Russian."

"Do you speak Russian, Joe?"

"No. Not really. Maybe a word or two. But I know the sound of Russian. This guy was definitely Russian."

"So, what do you make of that?"

"Probably one of those Russian Ollie Garks. Maybe a gangster. Who knows how these people get so much money. They had nothing, nothing; now they are buying everything. One of them wants to buy an American basketball team. What's next, baseball? They claim that they invented baseball. It's not right."

"You don't seem to like them much."

"No, I don't. They're a bunch of complainers. I could tell you stories."

"Another time perhaps. I'm going home to my husband. It's been a long day."

"Good night. Cheryl, right?"

"Yes, Cheryl."

"Well, good night, Cheryl."

ANTON VASILEVICH DASHKOV smiled often, and when he smiled, hearts froze. Stoekl never smiled and no one knew whether Stoekl was his given name or his family name, but, apparently, it was his only name. The documents from the orphanage that he spent his boyhood in simply bore the name "Stoekl."

Mo Sather stood in front of his own desk. Dashkov sat behind it, his small, chubby hands clasped in front of him. He was not a tall man, but he was powerfully built like an old-time fullback, thick arms, thick neck, and a large round head with only stubble for hair—stubble in at least three shades of gray that made his pate look like a map. He had very dark irises that hid the edges of his pupils. Stoekl was his opposite—very tall, with blonde, short-cropped hair and the muscles and heft of a tight end. He had big, soft hands and amber eyes that seemed to shine gold in certain lights. Stoekl stood behind and to the right of Sather, which made Sather very uncomfortable.

"I am not happy that I have had to clean up your dirt," Dashkov said in a monotone.

"I am sorry, Vassie. It was probably just an innocent mistake, the boy…"

"No matter. No more dirt, understood?"

"Yes, Vassie. We will clean up after ourselves next time."

"No. No next time. No dirt."

"Understood."

Mo Sather hated being talked to like he was a serf. He was sure that he was the most important architect in Boston and resented his treatment by this Russian thug and his lackey. Sather needed Dashkov's money, but he was already plotting his fall. Sather would play the fool and bide his time. The situation with the kid was an inconvenience, but it gave Sather all that he needed for the Feds.

"So, are you going to show me what you have done or just keep wasting my time?"

Sather reached out and picked up the handset of the conference room phone. He punched in three numbers and barked, "Come on. Let's go."

Five of Sather's staff filed into the conference room and four of them—three men and a woman—took seats along the wall, away from the table. A tall, thin man stood at four easels at the head of the table and turned three blank boards around revealing site plans, floor plans and elevations respectively. A fourth panel remained unturned.

The tall, thin man—Victor, although he never introduced himself—presented the site plans and floors plans in some detail, and, in his faintly Slavic accent, described entry points for people, cars and buses, as well as the features and amenities within the block-long project. The new buildings—set on a podium over a highway and train tracks—covered two thirds of the block, while the remaining third of the block was occupied by historic buildings along Newbury Street. Many of the historic buildings had recently been converted from stables to retail. These were to be maintained and integrated into the design of the complex, in part because City ordinances discouraged their demolition. Because of the topography and adjacent highway, the only on-grade access to the property was from Hereford Street and (via? by?) the land occupied by the buildings of the Boston Institute for Architecture. This property at the east end of the project site was colored a deep maroon on the site plans.

When Victor finished, he introduced Marta, a dark-haired woman who looked profoundly Greek, although she spoke with a mid-west American accent that evidenced her Ohio upbringing.

Marta revealed the final board, a bird's-eye rendering of the entire project at dusk, the last remaining threads of light behind sparse clouds in the background and lights twinkling in the windows of the three office buildings, capped by a strong glow from the top two floors of the tallest building. When she finished, she walked back toward her seat with her eyes cast to the floor.

"All told: One point six million square feet of office space, almost three quarters of a million square feet of retail on three floors and the most desirable and exclusive club in the city on the top of the tallest tower."

Sather's pride infected no one except Sather. The design team sat with plastic smiles. Dashkov was apparently unmoved.

"You may all depart now," Dashkov stated.

The smiles vanished and the five staff marched out the door after a brief shuffle of papers. No sooner had they left and Sather closed the door, when Dashkov leaned over the table and clasped his hands in front of him at arms length. "And the property of the BIA?"

"I'm working on it."

"I do not have infinite patience."

"Sixty days tops."

"What will happen in sixty days?"

"We will control the BIA board, the Dean and Holt can't stop us."

"You have forty-five days, then I will take my own action."

"It can't be done."

"Mister Sather, do not ever tell me what can't be done."

"Yes, Vassie."

"Are Piscara and Holt the only roadblocks? How can that be?"

"There are some on the board who won't vote against Piscara's wishes."

"And Holt?"

"He doesn't really control any votes, but he controls the discussion and he is close to Piscara."

"So it is Piscara who is the problem and it is Piscara who must be the solution. Good. We can dismiss any thoughts of Holt. One less complication."

"Yes, he is insignificant."

"Then why does he occupy you?"

"He is disrespectful. I will not be disrespected."

"Oh?"

The next morning, Bill Button sat on the sofa opposite his desk and read the transcript of the meeting in Sather's conference room. When he finished, he removed the front page and slipped the remaining pages into a brown envelope.

27

B EN SAT ACROSS THE SMALL TABLE FROM BLAIR
Winston, reading the two pages that Winston had given him.
When he finished he looked at the lawyer, removed and folded his read-
ing glasses, waited a long moment—apparently thinking—then spoke.

"Do you really think this will work?"

"Maybe long enough to make a difference."

"So you think a court would throw it out?"

"Fifty-fifty."

"Hmmm."

"Your best chance for it surviving a court challenge would be to
have the Board approve it and add it to the by-laws as a rule. That
might substantially improve your chances for making it stick."

"I'm not sure I have the votes. Am I right in assuming that if I
present it to the Board and it doesn't pass, my chances diminish sig-
nificantly?"

"Yes, in the sense that the Court would almost assuredly affirm the
Board vote, but that doesn't preclude you from implementing the rule
and letting the other side challenge it."

"Okay. One other issue: I am a candidate for re-election. Does that
create a conflict that will become a problem?"

"It certainly would create the potential for conflict, but—strictly
speaking—since the position is unpaid, it could be argued that there is
no basis for the conflict argument."

"Is that a winning premise?"

"On appeal perhaps, but unlikely before a Superior Court Judge who might see this as self-dealing."

"Thanks."

"Good luck, Ben. Now, how are Claudine and the family?"

"The family is well."

Winston peered into Ben's eyes and what he saw there scared him. "Do you want to talk about it?"

"Not yet. I'm working on something. I may need your legal advice down the road."

"Ben, sometimes the only course is love. Listen to her. Really listen to her. You can't solve everything yourself."

"Blair, I can't possibly admit that."

THE NEXT MORNING, Ben called the chair of the BIA's nominating committee and told her that he would not be a candidate for re-election. He then informed her that members who joined after the start of the current corporate year would not be eligible to vote in this election.

When the news got out, the reaction from the BIA and the wider architectural community was swift. By mid-afternoon, the number of messages into the Boston office of Satart Holt was mounting. The press was not to be left out and at least two camera crews from local stations had set themselves up outside Satart Holt's offices, just a block from the BIA.

WHILE THE STORM of messages grew, Ben and Claudine were making plans to fly back to Rio. It was time to say goodbye to Pascal and Severine and to send Daniel and Simone on their journey. Claudine asked that nothing be said about her illness until after Abeille was born. Ben agreed. He noticed that it was a request and not a demand.

He hoped that it signaled her trust in him, but he realized the full weight that that trust would bring.

"THE BASTARD! I won't stand for this." Mo Sather shook his fist in George Theroux' face.

"I've already called Carl Specks," Theroux said. "He'll prepare a motion to stay Holt's unilateral action. And I called Ed Kobans. He'll call an emergency meeting of the AAB's Executive Committee to take action against Holt. The board of Registration wants to wait to see how things work out. Oh, and Ellsworth Nelson stopped by, so I told him about Holt and he has offered to write a column about Holt's chicanery."

"Chicanery—that must have been Nelson's word. I like it."

Theroux looked crestfallen. He wondered why Sather thought that the term was Nelson's. It was, of course; but it could have been his, he thought, and to make matters worse, Sather loved it.

"Listen, Theroux, you go to the AAB meeting. I have another meeting that I need to do."

"Okay."

Sather took Theroux' arm and led him to the door. "Don't let the AAB vote some kind of effete swill. Make the members of the Executive Committee take a strong stand and make them agree to back our membership drive with applications from all of the staff from their offices. When Specks gets his injunction I want to punctuate it with an overwhelming mandate. Now go."

Sather nearly pushed Theroux through the door.

SATHER SAT AT his desk, raised the handset and spoke rather pleasantly. "Cheryl, please get me Mister Dashkov."

28

B EN CALLED JOSH HANLEY FROM THE TARMAC AT Hanscom Field just before boarding the plane to Rio. Claudine had already boarded.

"Hello, Josh," he said. "I wonder if you and your wife would like to come to Paris the week after next. Claudine and I will be there and there are a few people I would like you to meet. Have you or your wife been to Paris?"

"No, we haven't and I know that Diane would love to go. Let me check my schedule and see what I can do. She hasn't started her new job yet, so that shouldn't be a problem."

"Good. Let's talk tomorrow."

WHEN SATHER CALLED Dashkov, his call was intercepted by one of Dashkov's assistants. Sather had met a few of the young men who flitted around Dashkov with papers to sign, reports to read and always a ready Vodka. They all seemed to be copies from the same mold—tall trim, blonde and pretty. He had never seen one of them smile and, from the tone of his voice on the phone, this one wasn't smiling either.

"Mister Dashkov is unavailable for conversation. He will see you in his suite at New York Park Plaza Hotel tonight at nine p.m."

"Actually, it would only take a few minutes on the telephone now and we would be done."

"New York Park Plaza Hotel tonight at nine p.m."

"Okay. I can be there."

"Yes. Be there."

"CHERYL. I NEED to take the shuttle to New York this evening. And get me a room at the Park Plaza."

"Yes, Mister Sather."

29

AFTER FOUR WEEKS IN RIO, LEAVING FELT LIKE LEAV-
ing home. The children had made new friends. Claudine and
Severine had become sisters, and Pascal had settled into his role of
Grand Papah. Tears were shed, punctuated by hearty laughs and sea-
soned with plans to be together again soon.

Ben stood aside, observing the scene and remembering the same
scene played out in his own childhood. He had become the father of a
loving family. He wondered how it had happened. He looked to Daniel,
his arm draped around Simone's waist, and a combination of pride and
fear welled up in him—pride in his son's confidence and sense of right
and wrong, and fear for the adventure that Daniel and Simone were
embarking on. He knew that his challenge would be to protect them
without being seen. Gunter's people would be good at that. Daniel
would be livid if he knew.

Ben looked to Pascha and Emma. He watched them talk to each
other. He loved the people they had become. He watched Pascal and
Severine as they stood wrapped in each other's arms, swaying to some
unheard music.

Pascal had changed his life. He couldn't imagine what his life
would be like if he had never met Pascal. He was very happy that Pascal
had Severine, although it was impossible to look at Severine for long
without having impure thoughts. Her face was ageless, her neck long
and sleek and her figure thin but with noticeably round breasts. She

seemed to grow in Pascal's presence as Ben had grown alongside him. It made Ben sad to wonder how long he and Severine would have Pascal, which made him think of Claudine.

Ben watched Claudine talking. He thought of the day he first met her. Her hair was the same chestnut brown, her neck still long and sleek like Severine's, but her tall, thin body now carried Abeille in her swollen belly. Soon the baby would be born and the battle to save Claudine's life would begin.

JUST AS THEY were about to board the plane for the return to Paris, Ben got a call from Josh. He would come to Paris the next week. Diane would follow a few days later.

For Ben, it was the first sentence in what was likely to be a novel. Ben hoped that once he got Josh to Paris and showed him the facilities he was building for the research foundation, Josh would stay to lead the foundations work. He was glad that the story of the foundation had begun. He called Marcel and they planned a lunch with Josh for the day after he arrived. Marcel had made arrangements for Josh and Diane to stay at an apartment that he maintained for foreign executives visiting one of his companies. It was only steps from the building that he and Ben wanted to show Josh, located just a block from the area that included Pitie-Salpetriere Hospital, one of Paris' best.

The area was ripe for redevelopment, so the reconstruction of the building at 22-24 Rue Wallons to house Josh's labs was more than a personal quest; it was a good real estate decision.

30

IN THE MIDST OF PLANNING FOR THE REORGANIZATION of his architectural firm, Ben found himself—with much help frcm Marcel—planning the structure of the new company that would develop treatments from Josh's research. On Marcel's advice, the lab's headquarters would be in Lucerne, Switzerland, where a treatment center would also be located. The Paris labs would be close to several major hospitals besides Pitie-Salpetriere and included Pierre and Madame Curie Hospital, Cochin Hospital and Necker Hospital. The proximity of so many first-class hospitals would provide for a pool of experienced and accomplished researchers.

With Josh slotted as Director of Research, Ben turned his attention to the executive, financial and operations structure. Marcel agreed to be Vice-chair of the Board, if Ben would be Chair, and Ben penciled in Armando Lowell as CFO, though he was aware of Lowell's past role in Bernadine's investment firm. The investigation of the firm had never gained traction and both Marcel and Bill Button vouched for Lowell.

That left the question of finding a chief executive. Marcel was lobbying for Ben to take the job, but Ben resisted. He was in the midst of shedding responsibilities in his design firm. He didn't want to add more now. He also questioned his ability to lead a biomedical research organization. They were still tossing names around when

Charles Waxman announced that he was leaving the Boston research hospital where he had been hired to turn around an organization that had been failing fast. After three years of growing profitability, he wanted new challenges. If Waxman would agree, Ben had his CEO.

Ben tentatively named the organization "Fondation Bernadine Aubrey" and smiled at his own joke. Then he had second thoughts. When the name spilled from his lips, he wanted to take it back. He was about to apologize to Marcel for his bad taste when the old man burst into laughter.

"Brilliant. Wonderfully brilliant. I must admit to you that I still love Bernadine and miss her terribly, but this is perfect. It will really annoy her if this is successful and she learns that we are reinvesting all of the earnings, but she must be happy if its success saves Claudine's life."

Ben was about to laugh himself when Marcel's words struck him. As much as the research might save lives, Ben's sole goal was to save one life. Despondency struck him like a fist to the gut. When he got home he sat in the courtyard by the gong bent over, his head in his hands, his shoulders heaving. As he was finally about to rise from his seat and go into the house, his eyes caught the form of Claudine standing on the deck outside their bedroom on the top level of Marcel's house, beckoning him.

BEN AND CLAUDINE landed in Boston just as her water broke. Ben had arranged to have one of the Suburbans waiting, but now wondered if he was remiss in not ordering an ambulance. It was too late now, he realized, and they raced off with Claudine lying across the back seat, her head resting on Ben's lap.

Less than twenty-five minutes after arriving at Brigham and Women's Hospital, Abeille Claudine Holt was born—screaming, covered in mucus and utterly beautiful.

DURING THE WEEK that Claudine and Abeille spent in Boston resting for the return home to Paris, Ben spent two hours early each morning in the office and two hours after dinner at the BIA. The hours between, he spent talking to Claudine, rocking Abeille or working in his sketchbook on the designs for the renovation of the building that would become the Fondation Aubrey.

The restoration of the concrete walls would be the work of the building envelope consultant, as would the new rubber roofing, but Ben wanted to replace the old wood windows with new steel-framed windows with hidden fresh air vents on the upper two stories which would house the office areas. He cut a hole through the floors in the middle of the building, creating a three-story atrium capped with a glass roof whose framing referenced the framing of the glass roof on the old Les Halles markets.

The first floor housed the reception lobby, conference and presentation rooms, a café under the glass roof and a large gallery. Ben envisioned the gallery as an exhibit space for the foundation's technology as well as a space celebrating the lives that would be saved, as well as the scientists and technicians who saved them.

The labs were all to be located on two underground levels. This was to be the most technologically challenging part of the project. Extending the supports for the foundations and the interior columns would require drilling four holes at each column—one on each side—then filling the hole with a concrete slurry mix that encased a steel cage.

By the end of the week, the design was sufficiently complete to turn the drawing over to Josep and the Paris office staff. They would work with Jared Whiting and his staff on the building envelope issues.

THE WEEK AT the BIA was far less successful and satisfying. Specks had gotten his injunction and all of the new BIA members would be allowed to vote. Ben had second thoughts about his decision not to be a candidate for election to a third term as chairman of the BIA Board, but ultimately decided to let his decision stand.

He realized how good a decision it had been when Dean Piscara called for a special meeting of the Board to act on his motion to file an appeal of the judge's decision.

The meeting devolved into a circus bordering on farce. Sather had demanded that it be an open meeting and it was moved to Piscara Hall. The overflow crowd—mostly made up of the new members—spilled into an adjacent lounge and an audio feed was set up there.

After Ben called the meeting to order, Piscara rose to present his motion. Peter Pepper, a board member who still spoke with a heavy Swiss accent some forty years after leaving Switzerland as a teenager, spoke in favor of Piscara's motion and his right to make it. Then, without breaking stride, he spoke in support of the large firms buying memberships for their staff and their right to do so. Even Sather and Theroux looked bemused by Pepper's soliloquy. Andy Berman, a former student who represented the Alumni Association on the Board, spoke of the sanctity of BIA membership, but no one seemed to know where he stood on the issue of Piscara's motion.

Ben repeatedly interrupted speakers to try to keep the focus on the issue of the motion. Ellsworth Nelson sat in the front row of the audience, taking notes. Sather and Theroux said nothing, although at one point, Theroux seemed about to speak until Sather laid his hand on Theroux' forearm. Sather wanted nothing in the public record evidencing his intention of taking over control of the Board. His meeting with Dashkov earlier in the week had been unsettling and it was becoming clear to Sather that Dashkov did not consider himself bound by the niceties of reasoned debate.

When Sather protested that he was doing all that could be done and that Dashkov needed to be a bit more patient, Dashkov grabbed the placket of Sather's shirt and pulled his face to his. He spat his response. "What ever made you think that I am a patient man? You have until the end of the week to solve this problem or I'll have Stoekl solve it."

Stoekl raised his fist to Sather's head and jammed his extended finger behind Sather's ear. "Pop."

Dashkov smiled. "And Piscara will no longer be a problem."

THE VOTE OF the Board ended in a tie, but Ben, who as Chair normally didn't vote, added his vote and the motion passed by the slimmest possible margin. Berman called for reconsideration and the margin of victory for Ben and Piscara increased to three.

Sather sat silently, without apparent emotion. Dashkov and Stoekl would have to solve the problem. There would be no one to save Angel Piscara now. Sather was only slightly surprised that it didn't bother him.

31

B EN SLID THE PHOTOGRAPH FROM THE SMALL MANILA
envelope. It was wrapped in a thin tissue paper, which Ben peeled
back. A small piece of notepaper, folded in half, fell to the floor, and Ben
left it there while he looked at the picture. The boy was not smiling,
but he seemed happy. His dark eyes were set deeply in his dark skin
below a crop of curly, jet-black hair The effect was extraordinary—a
picture of a confident, handsome young man. Ben thought of Daniel.

Ben noticed a small reflection in the boy's right eye and took a
loupe from his desk drawer. He found the image of an equally dark
woman who, Ben thought, looked a lot like Severine with her long
neck and thin shoulders. The woman's facial features were hidden by a
camera held to her face, but Ben imagined she must be as beautiful as
the boy.

It seemed to Ben that the only thing this boy had inherited from
his father was a faint squareness to h_s jaw—a definite blessing for the
son.

TWO DAYS LATER, Ben handed the photograph to Carol LaPierre
and asked if she had seen the boy around the BIA. When she looked at
the photo she smiled a weak smile, then dropped the photo to the floor.

She pretended to fumble around for the photograph to gain some time to compose herself. Then she bent to pick it up.

"It's Ramone Cortes. He's a student here, or he was. He stopped attending classes a couple of months ago. He never withdrew though, so technically he's still a student."

"His real name is Carlos Y," Ben said. "And his father is looking for him. Do you have a home address?"

"I'll look it up for you. He filled out a student loan application."

"Good. How well did you know him?"

"What do you mean?" Carol challenged Ben. She fumbled her pen and it fell first to the desk before bouncing and landing on the floor. Carol didn't look at the pen but stared at Ben's face while avoiding eye contact.

Ben was surprised by the defensive tone in Carol's voice. "Did you take in his application yourself? Did you conduct the loan interview? Have you seen him around?"

"Yes, I did take his loan application and I did see him. He is very handsome. He would be hard to miss."

Ben thought that there was more, but decided that he could follow up on that later if he needed to. He would have Strout start an inquiry into the boy's apparent disappearance and he didn't want to harden Carol to Strout's inevitable questions.

"Can I get that address?" Ben asked again.

"Oh, yes, of course. Just a minute."

Carol went to a file drawer and pulled out a folder, opened it and wrote on a small note pad. "Here it is."

The address was 41 Union Park Street in the South End. Ben stuck the note in his pocket. He planned to stop by the address before he headed back to Paris.

32

MO SATHER SAT ALONE IS HIS CONFERENCE ROOM, contemplating the drawings set out before him. He whispered the question that was on his mind. "Is this wonderful project, as beautiful as it is, worth killing for?"

The answer came after a moment of introspection, an answer that shook the room's glass walls as he slammed his fist on the table. "You're damned right it is."

Dashkov and Stoekl walked along the edge of the surf at Revere Beach amongst the happy screams of darting children. After a long silence, Dashkov finally spoke. "I want you to take care of Piscara. Don't entrust it to one of your associates."

"Yes, of course."

"And I want Holt out of my hair, too."

"That will be done as well."

Dashkov swiped at a green-headed fly that buzzed his head. "What is your plan for Holt? You can't just shoot him. Even if you make it look like a botched robbery, Holt has too many friends that will ask questions, and they are used to getting answers. Obnoxious people."

"What do you wish?"

"I've been considering this. I think that we won't eliminate Holt, at least not directly."

"But Vassie, you said..."

"I said that I wanted him out of my hair. There are other ways to accomplish that. You need to think more, Stoekl, you know, be more creative."

"Yah, I don't do creative, Vassie."

"So listen to me."

33

"SO, WHY DO I HAVE THE HONOR OF A VISIT FROM the three of you together?" Ben asked without looking up from the papers he was signing. Strout and Button took seats on a sofa across from the conference table that Ben used as a desk. Gunter stood at the corner of the table, his arms crossed.

It was Bill Button who spoke first. "You asked Gunter to review Strout's reports. Strout's deep background came from me. We want to make sure that you take this seriously. This is a credible threat and probably an imminent threat."

"Tell me then—why would the Russian mob be interested in Piscara?"

"Dashkov is an independent. There doesn't appear to be any coordinated involvement with the Bratva, notwithstanding his claims to his associates. We think he's trying to show the brothers that he was able to launder money under the noses of the U. S. Treasury and the Justice Department. You don't need a psych profile to interpret the chatter we're hearing from him."

"So how does the BIA figure into all of this?"

Strout chimed in. "Because the BIA's campus is likely to be sold as part of a merger with BU. The BIA's property is the keystone in a development plan prepared by Mo Sather's firm. They already own most of the rest of the block through straws."

Strout flicked the switch on a projector and proceeded with a presentation outlining the properties Dashkov currently controlled, including those he owned, those under Purchase and Sales agreements and the one major piece of the puzzle still missing—the campus of the Boston Institute for Architecture.

When the presentation was over, the three visitors turned to Ben who was visibly shaken. They stared at him for a long moment before he spoke.

"So, what do we do?"

It was Gunter's turn to speak. "We need to increase the security around you, Claudine and the children. We need—rather, you need—to get Piscara to agree to protection. If you're not driving him home, we're driving him home. We'll also post one of our people in the BIA office, probably in the guise of a new staff member, maybe you need a secretary there."

"How much do we tell him?"

"As little as possible. Nothing about the development project. Nothing about Dashkov or Sather."

"How much does Sather know?"

Button spoke again. "Sather is in deep. We're not sure when he realized that his difficult, wealthy client had at least some ties to organized crime, but the chatter shows it has been a while. Gentlemen, I have to raise one wrinkle in the plans that you are laying out. Treasury wants this guy. They are not going to be happy if we use privileged information to draw a wall around Piscara. Any protection beyond Ben and his family's security is going to need to be transparent."

Ben said, "Bill, I appreciate your position on this, but that's not going to work. I can't be worried about Piscara when I'm away from Boston."

Strout stroked his chin. "I think I've got a cover story. We pass the word that Piscara has been stressed by the difficulties at the BIA and needs some assistance in getting around. His care workers can be a couple of Gunter's guys."

Ben and Button quickly agreed. In less than fifteen minutes they outlined a list of the remaining details to be worked out, then Ben stood up and asked that he be briefed on the plans once they were finalized. He asked Button to stay behind for a moment.

"Thanks Bill. I really appreciate the work you do, although you know I don't always like it."

"I don't always like it either."

Ben nodded. "Bill, I have a favor to ask of you, probably several steps below your pay grade, but I have been asked to help a father and his son." He pulled the small photograph from his jacket.

"Handsome boy. Who is he?"

"His father is Carlos Y. The son was enrolled at the BIA under the name Ramone Cortez, but he is Carlos Junior."

"Do you know who Carlos Y is? Where did you get this?" Button stared at Ben.

"From a worried dad. And, yes, I'm generally aware of Carlos Y's past."

"Be careful with him. I'll see what I can do. There may be side effects though."

"Daniel and his girlfriend are off on a long journey. They'll be gone months, maybe a year or more. He's looking for Bernadine. If we lose contact with him I won't care about the history of the person who helps find him and brings him home."

It was Bill's turn to nod. He hugged Ben. As he backed off, he looked into Ben's eyes, then turned and walked away.

34

CLAUDINE AND BEN SAT IN THE GARDEN AFTER DIN-
ner. Abeille was upstairs, being rocked in the Thonet rocking
chair that Ben had bought for Claudine when Daniel was born. Pascha
and Emma were out for an evening stroll with Marcel.

"Claudine, it's time we talked about your tumor and how we approach your recovery." Ben was sitting on a bench next to Claudine. He
didn't look at her but focused on the boxwood hedge that rimmed this
part of the garden.

"Ben, I'm afraid. I don't know what's happening, but sometimes
I feel that I don't want to know. I don't want to lose my memories. I
want to be here as my children grow." She stared at the side of Ben's
face, afraid of forgetting it, and continued staring at him as he turned
to face her. His eyes met hers, locking on to them for a long moment,
until he blinked.

"I know."

"I'm not sure that you do. You are never afraid."

Ben protested, "I don't think that's entirely true." He paused, took
a deep breath, then continued. "But let's not argue about that right
now. We need to develop a plan to evaluate your condition and consider
treatment options."

"I won't do anything that debilitates me and scares the children."

"Let's not get ahead of ourselves. First, we find out exactly what's going on in that beautiful head of yours, then together we work on a treatment plan."

"I want Isabel to stay involved."

"Okay, but remember that she isn't a neurologist or an oncologist. If you want her as a sounding board, that's fine."

"I trust her."

Ben turned away, looking to the boxwoods again.

"I know. There are a couple of other doctors and a researcher that I want you to meet, probably tomorrow or the day after. The researcher is in the process of moving here and I'll need to see how he and his wife are doing."

"Don't tell me that you have a researcher moving here for this." Claudine reached out and grabbed Ben's arm, turning him towards her.

"He's moving here because he's been offered a key position in a new biomedical research center that will be studying the use of new technologies for treating difficult illnesses."

"In Paris?" Claudine asked.

"Yes, near the hospitals."

"Where is he moving from?"

"The United States."

"Boston, perhaps?"

Ben could see that Claudine was seeing through his scheme. "Yes."

"Did you know him in Boston?

"I met him."

"Once? Twice? What do you know about him?"

"Enough! Marcel and I hired him. The new research center will be named for your mother."

Claudine laughed. "It is good to be loved by you." She threw her arms around Ben's neck and buried her face in his chest.

Ben smiled. He said to himself, "I hope so."

TWO DAYS LATER, Ben and Claudine prepared for their guests' arrival. Josh and his wife's apartment wasn't quite ready, so they would be staying at the Holt's home for a week or so.

Just after six that evening, Robert opened the door to the young-looking doctor and his wife, a lovely dark-haired woman considerably older than her husband. When they were settled in the sitting room, he called upstairs and announced to Claudine that the guests had arrived. He then went out to the garden to find Ben, before returning to prepare drinks for the visiting couple.

When Ben arrived from the garden, Claudine was already sitting in a winged chair and talking to Josh. When Ben entered the room, Josh stood to meet him. His wife sat facing Claudine with her back to Ben, her dark hair the only visible part of her above the chair back.

Josh stepped forward and offered his hand to Ben. After a firm handshake, he gestured to the woman in the chair and said, "May I introduce you to my wife, Diane."

Even before she rose to face him, Ben realized where he had seen that hair before.

"Oh, darling," Diane said. "Ben and I need no introduction."

Ben reached for Diane and drew her to him, enveloping her in his arms and holding her for a long moment before releasing her and kissing her on both cheeks. "Diane, it is so good to see you."

"Likewise, Ben. I never expected anything like this, but it seems so perfect."

"Sometime in the next few days we'll have to abandon these two and find some time to catch up."

Claudine turned to Josh. "Don't worry. I'll send Gunter with them, he'll keep an eye on them."

"I can't wait to hear this story," Josh said, with just a hint of jealousy.

35

A T ELEVEN O'CLOCK THAT EVENING, JUST AS THE last of the after-dinner drinks were finished, Robert summoned Ben to the telephone. "It's Blair Winston from Boston."

"Hello, Blair. Do you have news?"

"Not good news, I'm afraid, but not yet fatal." Blair Winston had a distinctly Beacon Hill accent, betraying the true Boston Brahmin that he was. "The judge granted them a partial injunction. The new members get to vote, although their votes will be counted separately until a three-judge panel can hear the case."

"How long before that happens?"

"Probably three to six months."

"Any guess on the outcome?"

"I wouldn't put a lot of money on it, either way, but I think that you're fighting an uphill battle."

"Well, let's fight it anyway."

"We will."

BILL BUTTON APPROACHED Ben while he was sitting alone at his table at Le Saint Germain, sipping on a hot, freshly-arrived allongé.

"Bad news, Ben."

"Good morning, Bill."

"Yeah, okay. Good morning to you, but not to the Misters Y, senior or junior."

"What have you got?"

"It looks like the kid in the picture you gave me is an unidentified young man who currently resides in the Boston morgue."

"Shit." Ben sat back in his chair, crossed him arms, took a deep breath and slowly exhaled.

"So, who gets to tell his old man that his kid is probably dead and that the Feds probably won't release the body because they have indicted the father and want him in custody? Tough message to deliver."

"Do the Feds know the identity of the kid?"

"Not that I'm aware, but..."

"But what?"

"I guess I'm still a Fed."

"You're a contractor now, a consultant. Right?"

"Maybe I need to check it with HR." Button grimaced.

"Don't you dare."

"Well, just so you realize that you are enticing me to break the law," Button smiled.

"You never needed much enticing, even when you *were* a Fed."

Bill shrugged.

Ben thought a moment. "We've got the cover that he was using the alias Ramone Cortes when he enrolled at the BIA. I'll grab his file. Let's look at it and see if his false identity needs any enhancement. I'm sure you can help with that. I'll have to tell Gunter. I'll need his help, but let's keep Strout out of it. I don't want to incriminate more people than we need to."

"Makes sense."

"I'll use my diplomatic ties to get him a French passport. We'll ask them to release the body to me as the French Consul in Boston."

"You're getting scary good at this," Bill said, nodding as he spoke.

"You've taught me well."

"I didn't know you were paying attention."

36

STOEKL WALKED INTO DASHKOV'S LIBRARY AND FOUND him sitting behind the huge desk. He walked up to one of the large winged chairs that sat in front of the desk and stood behind it.

"Stoekl. I want the Piscara thing to be taken care of without delay."

"It is already in the works."

"Good. I would rather that it was Sather, but you don't get to choose sometimes."

"We could make it so."

"No. Not for now. As they say 'Business before Pleasure'."

37

Time for a Change at the BIA
By Ellsworth Nelson

*T*HE QUESTION BEFORE YOU, DEAR READER, IS NOT *whether the Boston Institute for Architecture is among this great city's more beloved institutions, but whether the love affair has become stale.*

For more than a hundred years, the BIA has been a singular bastion for the common classes in the legendary battle with the Brahmins. Its character was born of fire, its mission to find a place for everyman in a world where the Ivy's excluded them. It was a war of honor and many were those who served with distinction.

Alas, the war is long over and the fires long quenched, but the Board of Directors led by its chairman, Ben Holt, and its dean of nearly six decades, Angel Piscara, continue to fight on in some vainglorious search for personal approbation.

Recently, a group of upstarts, itself helmed by some of the more successful and capable leaders of our architectural community, have tried to bring reason to the Institute's governance. Their efforts have been strangled in the dead of night by Messer Holt, who literally pocketed the membership applications of new voters.

We have witnessed the antics of Mister Holt before and your faithful correspondent has shed a clear light on his architectural thuggishness. His current bullying is, therefor, no surprise and the courts themselves have ruled that it cannot stand.

It is then left to the new, enlightened electors of this once great institution to throw out the bums—in the language of the streets from whence Mister Holt came—and bring new leadership to the service of the working classes. They may not create great, inspiring edifices, but their draughtsmanship is important to the work of those who do.

BEN LIKED READING the columns of Ellsworth Nelson, much as he liked listening to Paul Harvey. He might not agree with what they said, but he really enjoyed how they said it. As a bonus, when Nelson mentioned Ben's name, the office phones would ring and new work would come in.

38

STOEKL WALKED THROUGH THE FRONT DOOR OF THE split-level home, tripped over an ottoman inconveniently placed in the framed opening between the vestibule and the living room, flipped his brimmed hat onto a sofa and called out, "Honey, I'm home."

There was no response and Stoekl expected none. The house was rented through the end of the summer, when the owners would return from their trip to Germany and Austria.

Stoekl went into the kitchen and took a can of beer from the refrigerator, started to close the door, then reopened it to survey its contents: A jar of olives unopened, another half-empty, a vacuum-wrapped wedge of Muenster cheese and half a bratwurst. He took the half jar of olives and closed the door. He squeezed a paper bag containing half of a baguette and decided it was edible.

The light was all but gone from the sky when Stoekl sat in the cushioned wicker chair on the small patio. He set his dinner on the tiny table beside his chair and set a Leica camera with a compact telephoto lens under the chair. He was waiting for the last of the light to disappear before using the camera. He drank his beer, but never touched the olives or the bread. When the first beer was finished he stood up, crushed the can in one hand, then went to the kitchen and got another, popping open the can on the way back to the patio.

Within half an hour the sky was fully dark and the lights in the nearby houses shone brightly. Stoekl could clearly see Eda Piscara's dark features as she stood at her kitchen sink washing and singing. He raised the camera and snapped a half-dozen quick shots, then went back to his beer and waited.

Just before ten he could hear the closing of car doors on the road beyond the Piscaras' house. He moved quietly to the corner of the house and raised the camera towards the noise. As the bent old man tottered down the driveway, Stoekl could see the glow of lights that came on automatically. The man raised his right hand to his eyes to shade them.

"All of these brilliant architectural minds and not one of them found a way to stop blinding an old man!" Stoekl mused to himself.

Once Piscara was in the house, the lights on the car at the head of the driveway—a Jaguar—came on. As that car drove away, a second car—a black Suburban—followed, slowly at first with its headlights off, then picking up speed as the headlights came on.

Ben waited until Piscara had waved his usual left-handed salute, then he slipped the Jag into drive. He waited until Piscara had reached the doorway before driving away. About a hundred yards down the road, he saw the headlights on the Suburban come on. He had considered his constant tail an intrusion once, but it had now become a small comfort for him.

Gunter usually liked to be in the Suburban that followed Ben, but it was hard to justify when he had so much else to do. This night, the Suburban was manned by Ricardo, who had been with Gunter for years, and Jimmy, the new guy and an ex-boxer who was the son of one of Ben's childhood friends.

THE NEXT MORNING, Ricardo and Jimmy drove up to Salem to pick up a nurse—Annie Hatchett, and drive her to a meeting with Claudine and her physician, Isabel Deschamps, who had flown in from Paris especially to meet her.

ANNIE WAS SURPRISED when she had gotten the call from Claudine—no, not surprised, stunned. She had met Claudine once in the emergency room when the ambulance brought Don in, dead on arrival. They had spoken only briefly, but Annie had been touched by her grace and her concern for Ben. It had been a simple gesture—bringing him a glass of ice water—but a gesture full of a simple love that Annie recalled vividly now.

Claudine had been a bit secretive, Annie thought, and had not revealed the reason that she wanted to interview Annie in the company of her doctor who she referred to as "Isabel" or "Madame Deschamps." Even after all of these years of nursing, Annie always addressed a doctor as "Doctor"—even in the third person.

When she told Liz about the impending visit, Liz joked that maybe Claudine had found out that she had been Ben's high school girlfriend and had wanted to eliminate her competition.

"Don't be silly. If that were so, why would she bring a doctor?"

"Ah, but what kind of 'Doctor' is she?" Liz asked, setting off "doctor" with finger quotes.

39

WITHIN THE PAST WEEK, A FLURRY OF ACTIVITY kept Ben busy, both mentally and physically. Claudine announced that she wanted her own team—not just Isabel Deschamps—to review and vet the diagnostic tests and the treatment plans that Ben and Marcel's group had developed; the BIA held its election with the surprising result that the warring camps were divided fifty-fifty, which again made Ben the deciding vote until the new Chair was seated in two months; Ben met with several of Satart Holt's senior staff to talk about his plans for the firm; Bill, Strout and Gunter presented their plan for safe-guarding Piscara until the new board took over and he was, presumably, outvoted; and Ben claimed Carlos Junior's body and prepared to fly to Brazil to visit Carlos Senior.

BEN DECIDED TO fly to Rio alone—no security team, no Gunter. He counted on Claudine being too busy building her medical team to notice. Claudine was flying to Boston for an interview and Ben planned to be back home before Claudine returned.

ON THE FLIGHT to Rio, Ben wrote notes to each of his children, to Claudine and Marcel, and to Angel Piscara. He slid each of them into separate envelopes and placed them in a leather portfolio.

BEN DROVE THE rented black Suburban to his meeting with Carlos, parking it in front of the beachfront bar where they had first met. The same four men who were at the earlier meeting were again at a nearby table on the sidewalk. Five minutes after Ben arrived, Carlos walked up to the table and sat down just as Ben was rising to greet him.

"Is that yours?" Carlos asked, gesturing toward the Suburban.

"Rented."

"I'm sorry that I showed no manners in not being here to greet you, but there have been threats."

Ben nodded.

"So what brings you here, have you changed your mind about working with me?" Y asked.

Ben ignored the question. "I have brought you something."

"A gift perhaps?"

"The body of your son."

Ben saw the fingers of Carlos' hand stiffen, but there was no other outward sign of anger or emotion from him. After a long moment, the fingers relaxed.

"You are a brave man to come here like this. Where is Gunter?"

"Home, in Paris."

"So you came alone?"

"Yes."

"Is that not foolish?"

"I don't think so, and I don't think that one father brings another father the body of his son with an army."

"Do you know who did this?"

Ben slipped a manila folder across the table. Carlos opened the folder and removed the top sheet of paper. The paper bore many long black strokes that obscured parts of its text, but the answer to Carlos' question was there.

"You surprise me again."

"How's that?"

"You play the simple architect, a very smart architect to be sure, but how do you have access to this?"

"Strong family values."

"Of course."

Ben laid the keys to the Suburban in front of Carlos, then stood to leave. "I'm walking to Pascal's; your son is in the Suburban. Please don't get up. I'm sorry it wasn't a gift."

Carlos nodded. "But perhaps it is."

THE DAY BEN returned to Paris, he took Pascha, Emma and Abeille out for a long, meandering walk. Pascha reminded Ben that it had been a long time since their last *flaneur*.

"We should do *flaneur* more often, Father."

"Yes, we should indeed." Ben laid his hand on Pascha's right shoulder as they walked.

"Especially for the young ones."

Ben smiled. "Yes, especially for them."

After they had walked awhile, Ben asked, "Do you miss Daniel, Pascha?"

"Sometimes, but the house is full with Emma and Abeille." He seemed to be pondering a question. "Do you?"

"Yes, terribly, even with all the fullness in the house. Perhaps because of it."

Pascha slipped his left arm in Ben's right and they walked on, Abeille quietly gurgling in the Snugli at Ben's chest.

40

TUESDAY STARTED OUT TO BE A VERY BAD DAY. IT END-
ed much worse.

At six in the morning, Ben got a call from Jared and Paul recap-
ping a meeting of the senior staff that had just ended in New York. A
revolt was brewing that had originated in the Florida and California
offices. The senior staff there wanted more control, a bigger piece of
the profits and a path to a bigger percentage of the ownership. The two
senior staff that ran the Philadelphia office announced their intention to
quit and take the office's clients with them. The Boston and New York
offices were squarely behind Ben. Josep from the Paris office refused to
attend the hastily called meeting there, stating that he had the firm's
work to do.

Although the growing schism fell nearly along the lines of Ben's
plans for a reorganization, it upset him that he had waited too long and
that the breakup was being advanced by others.

WHILE STILL IN a disturbed mood from his morning phone call, Ben
went to Claudine's appointment with Isabel and Josh. They met at the
large conference table in Josh's office that had a large, unkept pile of
files and reports stacked at one end. The news from the testing that had
been done under Josh's direction was far beyond the worst that Ben had

anticipated, although Claudine seemed unperturbed, even calm, as she asked a half-dozen questions.

Claudine's brain cancer was growing, albeit slowly, but it was growing in an area that would soon make her unable to walk and eventually make her unable to breathe on her own. The cancer, Josh said solemnly, was inoperable.

Ben pushed Josh for a report on his research about the use of focused beam radiation to kill the cancer cells, but Josh was evasive. Great progress was being made, he said, and he was monitoring the work of others around the world who were also pursuing brain cancer research. There was a long way to go, but there was hope for an eventual cure.

"Yes, but when?" Ben demanded. "In time to help Claudine?"

Josh looked Ben in the eye, then his eyes fell to the floor. "No. I don't believe so."

"How much time do we have?"

Although the question came from Ben, Josh looked directly at Claudine when he spoke. "Maybe a couple of months until you'll need a wheelchair. We don't really know about the end. It could be a six months, maybe more, maybe less."

Ben spoke again. "Are we doing everything we can to speed up the research?"

"It's not an issue of speed. It's an issue of getting it right. It's not a matter of the efficacy of radiation, it's a matter of being able to target the tumor and leave the healthy cells alive. The problem is targeting, and the technology is not there yet. We have all the money we can use, thank you. We need to learn how to use it to solve all of the targeting issues and there are many. I know that this is important to you. It's important to me and to all the dedicated people working with us—and to everyone in the other research centers. We can't change the laws of physics; we need to learn how to work with them."

Ben stood and walked to the far end of Josh's large office. He looked out the window for nearly a full minute before returning and leaning on the table. "Josh, I know that it's important to you and I appreciate that, but right now all I want, all I need, is a solution. Nothing else means anything to me."

"Understood, but once again..."

"Let's meet again next week." Ben rose to his full height and reached out to Claudine who took his hand and rose alongside him. Isabel reached out and touched the back of Claudine's other hand. Claudine looked at her and smiled, then turned and walked away with Ben.

LATE THAT AFTERNOON, just as Ben and Claudine were returning from a walk, Robert informed them that Simone's mother was on the phone.

"*Bonjour*," Claudine said. She listened for a while, bobbing her head, but saying nothing, then abruptly extended the phone toward Ben. "Ben, can you talk to her?"

"What's going on?"

"Daniel and Simone are missing."

Ben took the phone and Claudine turned and walked slowly, silently up the stairs.

BEN FINISHED THE call, then he went upstairs and found Claudine lying face down on the bed. He sat on the bed beside her and brushed the hair off her cheek. He watched her soft, slow breathing interrupted by an infrequent murmur. At least she was asleep.

41

WHEN THE CLEANING LADY ARRIVED AT THE Lexington home, she parked at the bottom of the driveway and made an unholy clamor as she dragged a vacuum cleaner and two buckets from the back of the Dodge van. She was not an attractive woman, rather large and unseemly in her old two-sizes-too-large dress and her dark hair seeping from under some kind of turban-like head-dress. She seemed—to the neighbor across the street and another next door—to be vaguely Eastern European, but any Pole or Ukrainian could have immediately discerned she was Russian.

Either the people who rented the house were particularly fastidious or she was unusually incompetent, because she appeared every other day for almost a month. The only other person the neighbors had seen was a rather large and muscular man with a round, shaven head and a penchant for beautifully tailored dark suits. No one had ventured to the neighbor's home to meet its occupant. They had only seen him once, and that had been when it was nearly dark. The Payne's would be back just after the end of the summer and the renters would be gone anyway.

AS IT GREW closer to the end of the July, Stoekl grew more restless. He still wasn't ready to take Piscara and, unless something happened to the homeowners, they would soon be back and his intricately worked out plan would be dead. He knew that it was useless to try to push things from his end. He kept up his stoic façade while secretly, internally crying for action.

WITH ONLY THREE days left in the month, Dashkov had made his move. The financing deal with his partners had been sealed and Sather had finally cajoled enough directors of the BIA to sign the petition for a special meeting on the second day of the new month.

BEN WAS LIVID when he learned that ten directors had signed the petition for a special meeting of the BIA Board to discuss Sather's plan to merge the BIA into Boston University and to sell the property of the school in order to pay off the college's current debt and finance the merger. He knew that Sather controlled seven votes, but wanted to know where he had gotten the other three. He received no answer when he tried to call Missus Hartford and Dean Piscara, so he started calling each of the directors. Within two hours he had spoken to the three who had joined with Sather and argued with them and their sorry reasoning.

One director thought that it was only right that Sather should "Have his day in court." Ben had wanted to slap him and ask him where he thought Sather had been the last two months. One expressed surprised at the level of the school's debt and thought that the idea of a merger should be discussed, although he opposed it—probably. Ben had almost screamed at him, asking how he could have looked at financial reports and heard from the school's chief financial officer for the last two years and still not understand the school's financial condition. He was sorry, but the news was only sinking in now. The last of the three to sign the petition was a close friend and confidant of Piscara's and was the President of the Alumni Association. He was just tired, he said, of all of the arguing and bickering and the pressure from Sather. He had agreed to sign the petition so that Sather would leave him alone.

When Ben finally reached Missus Hartford later that day, he told her he wanted to meet with Piscara the next evening. They would meet at a local restaurant, Ciao Bella, and not at the BIA. He finished with a punctuation that startled her, "This is not a request!"

ON THE MORNING of his meeting with Piscara, Ben signed a letter that was to be distributed to every employee of Satart Holt, thanking them for their service, for their contribution of considerable talents to the work of the firm, and wishing them great future success in their endeavors. He then outlined the reorganization of the firm.

As soon as the letter was signed, and while it was being prepared for distribution in Blair Winston's mailroom, Ben started making phone walls.

First, he called the two senior staff that ran the Philadelphia office and fired them. He told them that the entire assets of the Philadelphia office, including the client list, were being sold to another Philadelphia firm headed by an old friend and classmate of Holt's. He also told them that security was on the way to escort them out.

Next, he called the head of the Florida office to tell her that she was fired and that the Florida office, the smallest of the offices and mostly doing residential work, which Ben despised, was being closed.

At ten o'clock, he met with the heads of the California offices and signed the papers selling the West Coast offices to them.

At eleven, he met with Jared Whiting and Paul Hogan, who headed the Boston, New York and DC offices and told them that they would share equally with Ben, Josep and Severine in a trust that would control sixty-one percent of the firm. The other thirty-nine percent would be held by an employee-owned trust. Pascal would share in the employee-owned trust. Jared objected to Pascal not having a full share of the controlling interest, but Ben told him that he had to fight with Pascal to get him to agree to even the share in the employee trust. Pascal was happy that Ben was pulling Severine back into the firm. He had worried that she was wasting too much of her time and talent taking care of him.

At noon, he met with Ellsworth Nelson, Nelson's publisher, the executive editor and business editor of the newspaper and laid out the story for them. When the meeting ended, the publisher stayed behind to assure Ben that the story would be written by the business editor, not Nelson.

"You can have anyone you wish write the story," Ben said.

"But you own the newspaper."

"One day, perhaps, but it is still Marcel's."

"What will you do when it is yours, or rather, your wife's?"

"We will talk about it when the time comes. If Claudine has her way, Nelson will hang from the flagpole in front of the offices. I'll probably have to convince her that that's not legal in the United States." Ben smiled, "Out of curiosity, how long have you been with the paper?"

"Thirty-two years. Twenty-two as publisher."

"Have you ever thought of owning your own paper?"

MOST OF THAT afternoon was spent with the security team, including Doug Strout, Bill Button, Gunter and two of his top people, Bruce and Jeanette. One outward change on the ground would be a second Suburban to deal with any attempted diversions.

"Will you tell Piscara about the security arrangements?" Strout asked.

Ben could see a suggested answer in Strout's eyes. "No, Strout, I don't suppose that I will."

Strout nodded. He knew then that Piscara was entirely unaware of the dangers he faced.

42

B EN WATCHED CLAUDINE AS SHE GOT OUT OF BED. IT was unusual for her to arise before him, but he had slept fitfully, slipping out of bed in the middle of the night to sit on the deck and watch the path that the moon took through the sky.

Ben had always liked to watch Claudine, appreciating her lithe body and the way her hair framed her head and punctuated her long neck. Now—and for the foreseeable future, he thought—he was watching for signs of difficulty walking, of pain in her neck and back, of any sign of weakness and the debilitation that Josh had forecast. He had so little time, he thought, and they had so far to go. He was alternately energized by the challenge and overwhelmed by the enormity of the problems that blocked a cure, but mostly he felt a crushing fear of losing her.

She smiled at him when she returned from the bathroom, then crawled under the covers and turned her back to him. "Hold me."

43

WHEN STOEKL WALKED INTO DASHKOV'S LIBRARY, he found Dashkov holding a large, heavy book open while dissertating on the work of Botero to a dark-skinned, dark-haired man casually but elegantly dressed in gray slacks, a crisp white shirt and a cream linen jacket. The man was nodding slowly as he took in Dashkov's lesson, never giving away the fact that he was the largest owner of the art of Botero in the world.

"Ah, Stoekl, good," Dashkov said. "This is Mister Carlos Y. We met some years ago at Madame Aubrey's on Bermuda."

"Mister Y." Stoekl reached out and shook Carlos' hand.

While the Colombian's hand was considerably smaller than Stoekl's, it matched the strength of Stoekl's grip.

"Mister Y is in town looking for his son," Dashkov continued. "The boy was an architecture student who seems to have dropped his studies and gone off on his own somewhere."

"Did he have a girlfriend here?" Stoekl asked.

"There you go. That's what I have told our friend. The boy is probably chasing after a girl."

"Perhaps." Carlos was carefully eyeing Stoekl. "Have we met before?"

"Unlikely." Stoekl turned and walked to a side table and poured a glass of water.

Dashkov said, "Well, Carlos, it has been good to see you again. I hope that you find your son soon. He's sure to show up and he will probably be embarrassed that he worried you. I'll walk you to the door."

WHEN DASHKOV RETURNED, Stoekl was sitting in a winged chair facing away from the door.

Dashkov walked past Stoekl and sat at his desk. "You'll have to add him to our list of problems to be solved."

"Why, Vassie? He's just a worried father looking for his son."

"His son is dead."

"What?"

"You don't need to know the details."

"Why would you have his son killed?"

"At the time I didn't know that he was Carlos Y's son. He worked for Sather under a false name. When Y showed me the son's picture, I recognized him from the newspaper story."

"He'll kill you when he finds out."

Dashkov stood, leaned across his desk and hissed at Stoekl. "Solve the problem before he does."

BEN WAS SITTING in the library in his Paris home when Robert burst into the room without knocking. Ben immediately knew that something serious had happened.

"Ben...it's Daniel." The butler pointed towards the telephone on the credenza.

"What about Daniel?"

"He is on the telephone for you."

Ben picked up the phone immediately. He wanted to yell into the receiver and demand to know where Daniel was, but he didn't. "Daniel."

"Ben. How are you?" There was a slight note of apprehension in Daniel's voice. Perhaps an apology, Ben thought.

"I got a lot better in the last few moments. Where are you?"

"India."

"Are you aware that there has been a search on for you and Simone?"

"Not until late last night. We happened to meet a French embassy attaché in a bar and we got talking and introduced ourselves. That's when we learned that you were looking for us."

"Are you both okay?"

"We're great. Sorry that we scared you all, but we were in Tibet at a monastery. Ben, it was wonderful."

"I know that you want to be independent, but let's make a deal. You pick the day and time, but we talk once a week. If you need to be out of touch for longer than that, you let us know ahead of time."

"I guess we can live with that."

Otherwise, next time I'm sending out the French Army, the American Navy and Gunter. Got it?'

"Got it."

"Have you found any sign of Bernadine?"

"We think so. We came across some good leads in China. We'll be heading back to Brazil and Colombia next week."

"I have someone who can help you if you want the help. I'll wait until you ask."

"Thanks, Pa-pa. We're sorry that we worried you. Can you tell the others?"

"Call Simone's mother. I'll tell Claudine."

"Goodbye, Ben."

"Goodbye. Be safe, Daniel."

44

ANNIE STOOD BEFORE THE AIRPORT DEPARTURE screen, scanning the listings.

"Eleventh down, Mom." Liz had come to see her mother off on her flight to Paris. "How long will you be gone?"

"Hopefully three months. I don't know how aggressive her cancer is, but they promised that I could come back for a week every three months."

"Are you afraid or anxious?"

"About what?"

"About being in a country you don't know for three months. About spending so much time with Ben? About Claudine dying? Gee, Mom, who wouldn't be anxious?"

"Actually, I'm surprisingly calm. I've got a job to do and it's a job that I'm good at—a job I love."

"And Ben?"

"You know, I thought that might be an issue. That's why I didn't say 'yes' to Claudine and Doctor Deschamps right away. Somehow it seems that I'm okay with it. I'm not sure why, but it seems natural."

"Well, good luck. I love you Mom."

"I love you, too. I'll call when I land."

Liz searched the terminal for a sign of her husband. "I don't know where Kevin got off to."

"Check the news-stand. He's probably got his nose in a book."

The two women hugged.

"Bye, Mom."

"Bye, Liz."

Liz watched as Annie walked away toward the gates. She hoped that her mother would stop and wave to her before she disappeared behind the security lines, but she didn't. Liz smiled to herself. Her mom was on a mission.

AT THAT MOMENT, Claudine, Ben and the family were gathered, along with Robert and Babette, in the large salon of their Paris home. Daniel and Simone were on the speakerphone. Claudine proceeded to describe her illness, the prognosis and the work that Josh and his team were doing to try to help her. She told them that she was optimistic and that she loved them.

"We'll come home immediately," Simone pledged.

"No. Live your life. I will live each day as well as I can; you must as well. That is what I want from all of you. That includes you, Ben."

"You *are* my life, Claudine."

"For now."

"Yes, exactly. For now."

AFTER THE TEARS and the embraces, Claudine announced that it was time for their first nightly *flaneur*, which they would do each night that they were together for as long as she could. They set out, wandering down to and along the Seine, watching the lights of the *Bateaux Mouches* as they slowly moved along the river.

As always, Gunter followed slowly in the black Suburban.

MUCH OF THE next morning, Ben spent time closeted with the lawyers who would arrange to transfer the ownership of Claudine's atelier and workshops to a company controlled by a new family trust. In what had started out as a show of support for Claudine—but which Ben had come to realize was a good business move on its own merit —Ben transferred all of his interest in Satart Holt to the same trust.

By early afternoon, Ben was making final preparations for a three-day trip to Boston to try to put an end to the conflict with Sather and his backers. He hoped to get a favorable court ruling in an appeals session before a single judge that was scheduled for the next morning, but—win or lose—he felt a new urgency to resolve the issues. He planned to offer Sather a bone by setting up a committee of twelve members with six appointed by Sather and the other six by Ben. He anticipated Sather's objection to appointing Angel Piscara to the committee and he was prepared to offer to withhold Piscara's participation.

Once on the road to Roissy, Ben realized he might be crossing paths with Annie who would be landing in Paris at about the same time Ben was taking off. He briefly looked out the window of the SUV, but realized he wouldn't be able to see her in any case. He sat back and wondered what their first meeting in so many years might be like, what she looked like now and what her life was like. He had told Claudine some time ago that Annie had been his high school girlfriend. The news hadn't visibly surprised Claudine and, when she'd asked if it had ended well, Ben had wrapped his arms around her. "For me, it ended spectacularly."

45

A S THE HUGE VEHICLE CARRYING ANNIE INCHED
along in Paris traffic towards Ben's home, she flipped through the
pages of one of several fashion magazines she'd bought at the airport
and fiddled with the cap of one of a half-dozen bottles of water that
sat in a small tub of ice on a console separating her seat from the one
adjacent.

"Would you like me to remove the cap for you, Madame?" The
driver turned in his seat even as the SUV moved ahead.

"No. No, I can do it." She struggled to turn the cap but it wouldn't
budge. Noticing that the driver was still looking at her, she silently
handed it to him and he removed the cap with a quick flick of his wrist.

"Thank you," she said.

"*De rien*—you're welcome."

She took a sip of water then picked up another magazine, this one
in German. As with the first, this one had a picture of Claudine on the
cover. She reached for another magazine and found the same. Soon she
would be caring for a woman she had admired—perhaps loved—for
many years. After the encounter at the hospital where Ben's brother
Don had been delivered already dead, Annie assumed that that was the
only time she would be so close to Claudine.

How strange it was that fate had proven her wrong.

Annie was looking forward to seeing Claudine again, but she
couldn't say the same for the prospect of seeing Ben. He must have

been aware of the arrangement Doctor Deschamps and Claudine had made. In the interviews—mostly by phone, but one in person—she had learned that Claudine knew she had been Ben's high school girlfriend. Claudine had known almost everything about her, including details she would have rather left unknown. Still, there was nothing criminal in her file and her troubles with her husband Harold were now dead and buried—literally.

She wondered again, for the umpteenth time, why Claudine had wanted her. When Annie had inquired as to how many other nurses she was considering, Claudine had told her there were none. "Why should there be? No, there is only you."

The Suburban pulled up in front of the carved dark-green doors at 11, rue Sebastien Bottin. The driver got out and came around to the rear passenger-side door, opening it and offering Annie his hand. Annie stepped down from the truck and mouthed a silent "thank you". As she approached the house the doors slowly, almost magically, opened to reveal a beautiful foyer. She stepped inside and looked up toward the top of the incredible space—an ornate central stairway rising three, no four, stories to a rosette skylight of stained glass. Annie was so immediately overwhelmed that she didn't notice Robert standing there, patiently waiting for the completion of a scene he had witnessed so many times before.

Thinking of the magazine covers and the few articles in the Suburban that were in English, she decided that this magical place was perfect as Claudine's home. Before the warmth of her reverie could settle in, she was struck by the realization that it was also Ben's home.

46

B EN WAS IN THE BOSTON OFFICE BY 6:10 THE NEXT
morning. He wanted to look through the notes on the divestment
of the West Coast offices that Marcel had written. Marcel was opposed
to Ben's dismantling of the Satart Holt organization, but he promised
Ben that he would advise him during the long process. It would take
three to five years before all of the intertwining relationships were un-
raveled. To Marcel that meant that there was no reason to proceed in
haste, but Ben insisted that the clock start immediately.

"At what point did I stop doing what I love and start doing
everything else?" Ben said. "I need to move on before it's too late."

After finishing Marcel's notes, Ben admired the wisdom and perception his father-in-law possessed. His advice tracked Ben's sympa-
thies—not his own. He was struck by Marcel's true selflessness and he
loved Marcel for it.

By 7:30, Ben was on the ferry to Lynn. He would have enjoyed a
breakfast meeting at the Capitol Diner, but the chances of the conversation being overheard were too risky. The meeting would be held in
the new penthouse that had been recently finished, but that was as yet
unoccupied, as Ben's Boston residence.

BILL BUTTON ARRIVED at the penthouse just before the 8:30 a.m. start time. Doug Strout was ten minutes late, as usual. Ben had asked Gunter to join them at nine, so they would have twenty minutes—thirty, if Strout ever showed up on time—for an intelligence debriefing.

Button started the discussion. "So, let's start with the cast of characters. We have Mo Sather leading a group of architects and engineers. He is clearly the figure in control of that group, which, by the way, includes George Theroux, the nominal head of the BIA. We have found no evidence that any of this group, with the singular exception of Sather, are aware of the tie-up with Dashkov and the parts of the Russian mob that are with him. They are an annoyingly, perhaps purposely, oblivious lot. As an aside, I have to tell you that I really despise their type."

"And they will continue to play oblivious when the house crashes around them. I share your disgust," Ben said.

"Then we have Dashkov and the people behind him. They are opportunists. They know exactly what Dashkov is capable of, but they see his operation as purely an investment. We know every one of them and are aware of their connection through the Russian dacha at Ozero. They control the oil and railroad industries, and this little investment is not much more than petty change for them, but with an outsized return. Dashkov is former KGB with a bad reputation for excessive brutality even among his brutal colleagues. After the collapse of the Soviet Union, he became a mid-level player in the Russian mob until he moved to Austria and became a marginally legitimate investor with a tendency toward old habits. Interpol and the U.S. have been trying to pin the mysterious disappearances of some former business partners on him with little real success."

"And what about Dashkov's right hand man? What's his name?" Ben said.

"Stoekl. We have nothing to report on him yet."

"Why is that, Bill?" Ben wondered what Button knew, but wasn't saying.

Strout interjected. "That's the strangest part of this whole operation. I have tried every source I have and we don't know anything about him. We don't know who he is, what he does, where he comes from. He's an enigma. The most that I've been able to get is a phone number, but I can find no information on who the number belongs to or whether it's in use. If you call it, you get nothing but a beep. For an answering device? It was once a number connected to a throwaway, pre-paid phone that expired two years ago. I'll tell you, our guys should be so good."

"But this guy is real, right?" Ben asked, raising his eyebrows and splaying his hands in front of him.

"Oh, yes. We've seen him. We've heard him on surveillance recordings. He is very real." Bill nodded as he spoke.

"Anything else regarding the cast of characters?"

"Nothing except your cast of characters at the BIA. They all appear legitimate. Some may be under the influence of Sather, but that's more stupidity or wishful thinking then any form of criminal intent. The same is true with the AAB. No sense of the real world, but that's not criminal, although I could argue that it should be."

Strout interrupted again. "The odd thing about Sather is that no one likes him. Piscara threw him out of a teaching position at the BIA years ago, yet he's back. Why?"

"I wish I knew, Doug," Ben said. "I'm as bemused as you are about Sather. And what do we hear about Dashkov's next move. Is he willing to let Sather try to gain control of the Board and, eventually, the property? I wouldn't bet against him pulling it off."

Button spoke. "We don't think he's going to wait. The chatter indicates that a move against Piscara is imminent. Perhaps, you as well."

Strout nodded. "He's not a patient man and the money behind him wants to be spent or the pockets will move on."

"Timing?"

"Not sure. We're tracking."

"Months? Weeks? Days?"

"Days."

47

JUDGE BRIAN WILCOX HAD SERVED ON THE U. S. District Court bench in Boston for some thirty years. He looked like a judge, he thought like a judge, he spoke like a judge. Ben had known Wilcox when the latter was a young attorney in the Massachusetts Attorney General's office, serving under Scott Harshbarger. Ben hadn't realized it then, but reflecting now, he thought that Wilcox had seemed like the perfect model for a judge, even then.

Wilcox was handsome, with a square jaw, Brahmin nose and black hair. There had been flurries of gray in his hair back when Ben had known him—when the judge had been in his thirties—but the flurries of gray were gone now, benefitting from a regular visit to a salon, Ben guessed. Like Harshbarger, he had an athletic build and, although he was quite a bit taller than his boss, seeing one reminded you of the other.

THE PARTIES AND their attorneys gathered in the judge's antechamber. Ben's side consisted of himself, Blair Winston and Angelo Piscara. Sather's side included himself, Russell Higgins, Scoot Peabody, George Theroux and their attorney, Carl Specks. The two camps stood on either side of the fairly large room, which was furnished with two wooden desks each occupied by a middle-aged secretary, several shelves filled with law reference books, file cabinets that matched the shelving, and four visitor's chairs in a semi-circle between the desks.

They had only waited ten minutes or so when the judge's senior clerk and a young junior clerk emerged from the judge's chambers.

The younger clerk said, "The judge will see you in a moment, but he only wants to see the attorneys, Mister Holt and Mister Theroux."

Sather exploded, "But I'm the plaintiff here!"

"Judge Wilcox will issue his written ruling after the conference, but I can tell you he is prepared to rule that you, Mister Sather, have no standing in this case."

Ben turned to Piscara. "Will you be okay sitting here by yourself?"

"Maybe I'll take a walk."

"No. Please just sit here."

"I will not sit in this room with Sather."

The junior clerk turned to one of the secretaries. "Miss Hartford, would you take Dean Piscara to the café for an espresso?"

"Yes, of course."

Picara's eyebrows arched, but otherwise his expression was blank when he asked, "Are you, by any chance, related to my secretary, Emily Hartford?"

"Yes, she is my cousin."

The Dean allowed Miss Hartford to take his arm and guide him from the room.

As they left, Piscara could be clearly heard. "He is an evil man, you know."

AFTER EVERYONE WAS seated, Judge Wilcox kneaded his brow, lowered his hand to his desk and spoke. "I will be ruling in favor of the defendants, Messers Holt and Piscara, but I think it to be a Pyrrhic victory unless the parties are able to come together and work out a reasonable compromise.

"Here is the reasoning behind my decision. While there are no specific rules in the BIA's by-laws regarding the timing and qualification of voting memberships, and the lack thereof might be construed in favor of the plaintiffs, I find a plentitude of collegiality in the intent of the framers. Indeed the BIA was originally founded as a consortium of like-minded architects intent on offering training and education to those who hungered to join their ranks. The BIA's tradition of a volunteer faculty evidences that spirit of collegiality.

"Mister Holt acted to extend that tradition. He did not, in fact ban or deny the proposed memberships, did not materially deny their voting privileges, but simply deferred them.

"Since the by-laws allow the Membership Committee to review potential candidates for membership, Mister Holt's scheduling of such review for a time certain, albeit after the elections, was not egregious.

"Ruling for the Defendant."

The judge stood and the parties in the room stood, as well.

"I hope that you take my words about compromise to heart. The BIA is an old and honored institution. I'd like to see it thrive in that collegial spirit that formed the basis for my ruling.

"Now, get out of my chambers."

THAT NIGHT, BEN attended a meeting in a church basement in Newton Corner with the three Newton Aldermen from Newton Corner—two from Newtonville, and one who was the chair of the land use committee of the aldermen and about fifty-five neighbors from Newton Corner, Newtonville and West Newton.

Tony Ramp, the chair of the Newton Corner Neighborhood Association presided and introduced Ben who proceeded to describe the two projects—in Newtonville and Newton Corner—that he and his group had envisioned. After he finished, Ramp asked for questions from the crowd. The land use committee chair stood up and told the neighbors of the process that the Board of Aldermen would implement for the review of the project. He suggested that there might be as many as three public hearings and a number of working sessions, estimating that the review would take the better part of a year, even though the law required that it be completed in about six months. When a couple of the neighbors asked how they could take a year if the law required a decision in six months, the alderman responded that the applicant could collect a denial in six months, but might want to ask the aldermen to waive the six month requirement in order to seek a better outcome.

Several of the neighbors snickered.

At first, no one in the audience seemed to have any questions. Then one asked whether Ben had considered housing on the Newton Corner site.

"We have proposed some housing along the outside of the ring road, but we are skeptical about housing on the air-rights due to the cost of the platform. The housing would have to be in a building that we consider to be too tall and which would cast unfortunate shadows over the neighborhood north of the turnpike, so we did not place housing there."

The floodgates opened.

"I don't see why you have to build anything taller than two-story town-houses over the turnpike."

"My father was a developer, he could have done something smaller here."

"I like the shops as long as they are local."

"I want to move my donut shop there. Will the rents be low?"

"The project is too big."

"No, the project is too small. We need the tax money to keep the library in Newton Corner."

"There is probably Federal money available to build a park over the Turnpike."

"Yes, let's build a park and a parking garage for commuters so that they don't park in front of my driveway."

In the end, the neighbors voted to ask the aldermen to look at the possibility of building a park over the turnpike.

Ben packed up his drawings. Marc Lipoff apologized and suggested that they try again in a few months after he worked with the City to build a consensus for the project. He said he thought that the project Ben envisioned was worth fighting for.

Ben smiled. "Marc, I have more fights than I need right now. Let me know if things change. The community needs to think about what it wants and how it wants to get there. We've started the dialog. It's up to you now."

"I hope that you're not discouraged."

"No, but I'm pragmatic. There is a great leap between a park or townhouses and the extent of development required to be economically feasible. Someone has to be the leader here. It's not me."

48

THE BLACK SUV WITH DARK, TINTED WINDOWS emerged from the gated compound and sped to a small, private airstrip some twelve miles away. The driver, Rachel, was a tall, trim woman.

Carlos Y looked through the rear right window intently, but saw nothing outside.

They had barely arrived at the single runway strip when the large doors of a hanger slid open and the short, stout tug easily pulled a small jet out onto the apron. There were another four or five planes left behind in the hanger and another three identical hangers clustered around the runway's midpoint. There were no other planes in sight.

"Please thank Bernadine for me, Rachel." Carlos handed Rachel a thick envelope, then turned and walked to the jet as the stairway was lowered into position. He climbed to the top of the stairs, then stopped and turned to look one last time at the SUV, but it was gone.

After the jet left Russian airspace, it turned north, heading along the polar route to its destination.

BEN MADE SEVERAL calls over two days to Mo Sather's office and left several messages.

None of his calls were returned.

HIS LAST CALL with Dashkov had left Mo Sather badly shaken. After sitting in his office alone with the door closed for the better part of an hour, he suddenly stood and, leaving his hat and coat behind, walked from his firm's offices. He declined the first elevator that stopped on his floor because there were three people inside and then took the next elevator alone. Once outside, he hailed a taxi, but rejected the first and took the second. He had the taxi pull halfway onto the sidewalk at the front door of his Beacon Hill townhouse, then emerged from the cab and walked quickly to his front door.

THAT EVENING BEN called Claudine. After talking to Pascha and Emma, he made googling baby sounds to Abeille, then talked to Claudine for an hour and a half about the family and the changes occurring in their daily routines.

Daniel had called. He and Simone were leaving Argentina, would stop to see Pascal and Severine in Brazil, then fly by way of Morocco to eastern Europe, probably spending some time in Moscow and, perhaps, Saint Petersburg.

Annie was settling in. She was enjoying Paris and was delighted to be reunited with Diane. The apartment that Ben had assigned her in Diane and Josh's building was perfect for her, she said. She loved the space under the eaves on the top floor and loved the rooftops and steeples that she could see from her windows.

"That is not a surprise, no?" Claudine said. "Doesn't everyone love Paris?"

"Yes," Ben said. "Paris is an easy place to love. I hope that she takes some time, while she can, to explore a bit. We'll be putting a lot of demands on her soon. How are the two of you getting along?"

"I don't understand 'getting along'," Claudine said.

"Do you like her?"

"Oh, yes, very much. She seems very nice and very caring. She makes hard questions seem so easy. It makes me think, though."

"About?"

"About what you must have done to lose her."

Ben briefly thought about telling Claudine the story, but thought better of it. "Probably all of the same things that I have done to lose you, but you refuse to be lost."

"You tortured her the same way you have tortured me? You bad boy. You must come home now."

"Believe me there is nothing I would like better."

"I miss you."

"When I'm done here I'll be around so much that you'll remember the days you missed me fondly."

"Never."

"Trust me."

49

DASHKOV WAS IRRITATED THAT STOEKL COULDN'T BE found, but he was determined to proceed immediately with his plan. The BIA had called for a special board meeting a week from that night. He wanted to be sure that the votes were in place to move forward with the sale of the BIA property. His investors were impatient.

The bound offering prospectus lay open before him. Dashkov had looked briefly at the plans and renderings, the photographs of the model and the summary of the buildings to be built—hotels, apartments, retail shops and offices that would change an entire block in the Back Bay and enrich Dashkov and his partners gloriously. Alas, it wasn't the drawings that excited Dashkov; it was the financial analysis pages that lay open before him. They attested to the enormous wealth and prestige that this project would bring him. He would finally be counted among the oligarchs. No longer would he be dismissed as a mere servant to the biggest of them; he would be their equal, or better.

BILL BUTTON CALLED an emergency meeting of the security team, including Doug Strout and Gunter, as well as Bruce and Jeanette. They met in the one-story garage that housed the fleet of black Suburbans and two black Mercedes that were used by the Holt's security staff.

"We have had an exceptional pickup in communications traffic between Dashkov and his partners. Two new players have come to the table and both of them have Russian mob ties. Both are involved with brutal crime groups in eastern Europe."

Button distributed grainy photographs of the two men. As he finished, he adjusted his eye-patch and smoothed back his sparse gray hair in the same motion. His wrinkled standard-issue trench coat smelled of yesterday's cigar—undoubtedly Cuban. "Sorry, but this is the best we've got. They're from surveillance cameras so they're not the best. The shaven-headed man is Dimitri Dimistriev. All of his gang members are similarly shaven and have a tattoo on the back of their heads that is the Russian word for 'silence'. The crew-cut man is only known to us as Lev. He is a former army commando and former prison guard in a system that was notorious for its lack of ex-cons."

Jeanette raised her hand, then lowered it quickly. She was very aware that her fingers were far too long and thin—too feminine—for her job.

"Yes, Jeanette."

"Will we be looking for back-up from the Feds?"

"Treasury is 'looking into the activities of Mister Dashkov and we are very interested in him.' That's their quote. By the time they are in, we may have some bodies."

"No FBI?"

"No, they say it's Treasury's investigation."

"Can we expect any support from the Staties or the local police?"

"If we have a live incident—a funny term for a situation where people die, isn't it?—then they'll show up. Our job is obviously to prevent a 'live incident'."

Strout raised his head from his hands where it had rested for much of the meeting.

Bill looked to the older man—a man that Button thought was too old for this work. He wanted to say "Why don't you retire, old man?" Instead he said, "What is your plan?"

Strout responded. "Gunter and I had a preferred plan which had him driving a Suburban carrying Ben and Piscara, but Ben nixed it, so we have a back-up. The first Suburban, with Gunter in it, will arrive just ahead of Ben's Jag. He will do a visual clearance of the area and pull up one hundred yards ahead of Piscara's driveway. Bruce and Jeanette will follow behind the Jag and park one hundred yards behind Ben. Bill, you will be in the last car and will drop back about five hundred yards or so and be our eyes from that direction.

Jeanette raised her hand again. "When?"

Strout answered, pulling his nylon golf jacket across his ample, but solid belly. "Next Tuesday night, Ben is meeting with Piscara and the directors who are solidly against the sale. He will be driving Piscara home after the meeting."

"And after that?"

"There is no other meeting scheduled before the special Board meeting at the end of the week, but that may change. If it does we'll have to do this all over again. After the Board meeting, I would expect the interest in Piscara to wane, no matter which way the vote goes."

"So a week of high alert and unbearable tension?" Jeanette said, biting her lower lip.

"That's about it."

All but Strout and Button nodded.

Bruce asked, "You okay with this, Strout?"

"I'm an old man," he said. "And I'd like to get a whole lot older."

"So would we all. My question is—are you okay with this?"

"I'm in. I was always in, but I don't have to like it. Greed! It's worse than religion at killing folks." Strout pulled his baseball cap onto his head and walked from the garage, not looking lack at the others.

BEN WAS BECOMING increasingly frustrated. There were less than two weeks left before the board meeting and nothing was happening. Sather was nowhere to be found and the rest of his people were intentionally unavailable. At least the ASB representative on the Board was willing to tell Ben that she would have nothing to say until she spoke with Sather.

With six days remaining before the meeting with his group of solid votes and nine days before the board meeting, Ben made the decision to fly back to Paris. He flew out of Hanscom Field in Bedford, just outside of Boston, so that he might avoid prying eyes. He called Button and Strout from the plane as it cleared the Maine coast. He had Jeanette with him, having told Gunter of his plan as soon as he'd made the decision. He suggested that Gunter stay behind lest someone put together the fact that Ben and Gunter were out of sight at the same time.

IMMEDIATELY AFTER LANDING at Orly, Ben headed home in a cab. When he walked through the door at Sebastien Bottin, it was just after six in the morning. He made himself a cup of coffee and grabbed half a baguette from the previous day and went out into the garden.

His first sip of the coffee reminded him of how valuable Babette was.

BEN SPENT THE next day and a half with Claudine and the children. He lost all interest in the BIA, the ASB, Sather and the whole mess. A small voice in his mind argued that he should just drop out, leave all of these fools to fend for themselves. But then he thought of Piscara. Piscara was the keystone to the BIA and to Ben. It was Piscara who sent him to Paris. From that act of kindness had come all that Ben had now.

No. He could not run away to hide behind this glorious façade. He had to see this through.

50

L ATE IN THE AFTERNOON OF HIS SECOND DAY HOME, Ben took a long leisurely stroll through the Seventh Arrondissement with Claudine and the children. He carried Abeille in a sling. It was getting difficult for Claudine to walk, so she clung to Ben's free arm.

At one point, Ben noticed Pascha and Emma walking ahead of him, deep in conversation. While he could only hear some of what they were saying to each other, the maturity of their conversation struck him. He realized then that he and Claudine had somehow raised a good family. The thought, he hoped, might sustain him in the days ahead.

That afternoon Ben met Annie as she arrived to spend some time doing fine motor exercises with Claudine. It had been more that twenty-five years since that night he'd last seen her. He had expected some tension when they met for the first time since the break-up, but there was none. Annie seemed genuinely happy to see him and he had to admit—at least to himself—that it was nice seeing her. They talked for some twenty minutes before Annie excused herself to attend to Claudine. When Annie talked Ben saw a dancing light in her eyes. He couldn't recall if it had always been there, but he liked it. For her part, Annie noticed how confident Ben had become. It was quite sexy. It had been a long journey, she thought, from the Brickyards to Paris and Ben wore it well.

They talked about family—Annie had a boy and a girl. The girl was getting married soon; she was hoping that the boy would settle down with a nice girl. Annie told Ben that she enjoyed meeting Pascha and Emma, and the baby Abeille, and that she was looking forward to meeting Daniel. She said that she loved Ben's home. Ben quickly pointed out that it had been Claudine's when they'd met and that his only contributions had been the redesign of the gardens and the alterations to the top floor.

Annie laid her hand on Ben's forearm. "Those are the most beautiful parts of this house. I always knew that you would be making beautiful things."

"Well, I…"

"Just say 'thank you'."

AFTER ANNIE WALKED away, Ben thought for a moment, then whispered to himself. "I am in this house with the only two women I have ever loved."

THE NEXT AFTERNOON, Ben made several calls to Boston from his desk in the library and found that little had changed. No one had seen Sather and his people refused to talk without him. The only news of any interest was that Carlos Y had called to thank him for his service and hoped to see Ben in Rio soon.

Ben smiled. He hadn't told Button or Strout what he had done with the reports on Y's son's murder. He was hoping that Carlos would be his trump card.

WITH NO OTHER news at hand, Ben decided to stay in Paris until the last moment. If he left by late afternoon the day of the first meeting, he could be in Boston by five or five-thirty East Coast time. He and Claudine had a late lunch in the garden, then Ben headed to Orly. He hoped to return late on the night after the Board meeting and enjoy a very long, uninterrupted stay back in Paris.

AFTER BEN ARRIVED in Boston, he spent much of the daytime hours in his office on Commonwealth Avenue. The pile of paperwork seemed insurmountable, but by just after four-thirty that afternoon, the pile had become small enough that he decided to quit for the day and head over to the BIA.

An hour before the Board meeting, Ben arrived at the BIA to meet with Dean Piscara. It was a meeting he was not looking forward to. Ben needed to convince Piscara that he should remain calm and silent during the Board meeting. The Dean's message on the merger and the sale would be delivered by others.

He knew that his entreaty to Piscara was likely to fall on deaf ears. It wasn't that the Dean was mean or combative, but he was obstinate, and his advanced age—he would be ninety-six just days after the meeting—didn't help. It seemed that the Dean was literally becoming deaf.

Hezekiah Wilson had been selected to present the argument, supported by the Dean, that the BIA should continue on as an independent school and that, in doing so, the issue of selling the property would be moot. Ben liked the clear unburdened argument that Wilson's words carried. There was also the advantage that no one could overtly dislike Wilson. He was thoughtful and quiet, speaking only when he could contribute light to an argument, never fire. His bushy mustache and shaggy hair gave him the look of a child's plush toy. Anyone who directly attacked Wilson risked looking churlish.

The Dean liked Wilson and agreed to hold his own arguments until he saw where the flow of the meeting was going. "But I will not be silenced, not by anyone, not by you,' he had told Ben. "One can never be silent in the face of evil."

"Do your best," Ben told him. "Let others make the arguments. Be the one that brings wisdom to the table, not bullets."

"So you're asking me to be the old man. I won't do it."

"You *are* the old man. I'm asking you to be the wise man."

"Who will be speaking?"

"So far five people have asked for time. Wilson, of course; Andy Berman from the Alumni; Mike Interbartolo; Peter Pepper, and from the other side, Ed Kobans, the ASB President and Richard Nolan, the ASB Executive Director."

"No Sather?"

"I haven't heard from Sather, but I'm sure he'll have something to say. I haven't heard from Neil either. As the BIA treasurer I'm sure he'll have something to add. He's solidly in the Sather camp."

"Why are you letting Pepper speak? He'll pull one of his verbal journeys that will lead him into some intellectual trap that he won't realize he's in. When he's done no one will have any idea where he's gone, especially him."

"I know, but I couldn't dissuade him, and he might just confuse them enough that they don't know what way they're voting."

"You're joking, I hope."

"Yes, I am indeed."

"Just tell him to be quiet."

"It wouldn't work with you."

"No, Holt. No, it won't."

TEN MINUTES BEFORE the scheduled start of the meeting, Ben and Angel Piscara entered the elevator for the ride to the sixth floor. The night before, Ben had had a dream in which Sather and a few of his supporters had entered the elevator immediately behind them and Sather had said hello to the Dean who had immediately launched into a fiery argument in support of the BIA's continued independence. He'd awoken before Sather had been able to respond. He was glad that the elevator was now empty except for himself and the Dean.

FOR HALF AN hour, eight men and two women sat around the Board table waiting for all—or at least most—of the other eleven members to appear.

"Well," Ben said, looking along both sides of the Board table, catching the eyes of each of the assembled directors. "We've waited as long as reasonably possible for the others to appear. Let's get started. Will the secretary please call the roll?" He looked to Carol LaPierre, who took the minutes at all of the Board meetings.

"Point of order, Mister Chairman," Board member Peter Pepper said.

"Yes, Peter." Ben wondered whether Peter could sense the exasperation in his voice.

"I want to raise the question as to whether there is a quorum."

"Why?"

"Why? Mister Chairman, the by-laws state that a quorum shall be one-half the sitting members plus one. I believe that means that we need twelve members here and we only have ten."

"No. I mean why, because the by-laws also state that any member can question whether there is a quorum. If no member questions the quorum, the meeting can go forward."

"But is that intellectually honest?"

"It doesn't matter now. You have raised the question. The Chair is duty-bound to rule on the question and I rule that there is not a quorum. Thank you, Peter."

"Shouldn't we put it to a vote?"

"Do you want to vote on whether the Chair is able to count?"

"No. Shouldn't we vote on whether there is a quorum?"

"Read the rest of your by-laws, Mister Pepper. The Chair must rule as to whether there is a quorum. It is not votable. This meeting is over."

Ben turned to the Dean and told him that they could head home early. The Dean had his head in his hands. Ben saw that he was trembling and thought he might be crying, but when the old man lifted his head, Ben realized he was laughing. Ben laughed too.

Pepper approached and explained that he hadn't wanted the meeting to end; that he'd simply wanted the Board to vote that it should go forward despite the lack of a quorum.

"Peter, do you drive a screw with a hammer?", Ben draped his arm over the shorter man's shoulder.

Peter looked confused.

"Don't think about too much, Peter. I'm sure you can make an effectively effete argument that a hammer might be a more efficient screwdriver."

BEN'S HOPE OF getting home early was dashed by a request for a strategy session by two of the Board members, including Pepper. By the time Pepper had finished offering his off-the-cuff evaluation of strategy alternatives, they had arrived at the time the Board meeting had originally been scheduled to finish.

"Peter, the Dean and I are going home. If you and the others want to keep this up, go ahead without us." Ben stood to leave.

Pepper wanted to go on, but the others took the opportunity to say their good nights.

51

"THERE SEEMS TO BE A CONVENTION OF BLACK trucks going on," Piscara observed as they left the BIA's main building. The street was wet from an earlier rain and the wet asphalt seemed to multiply the number of headlights on the lined-up SUV's.

Ben decided not to lie to Piscara. "They're my people. Security. Though, since the other side didn't show up tonight, maybe they've thrown in the towel. I have to admit, it doesn't seem like Sather, though."

"I think that you are over-worrying things. We're in Boston, you don't need that much security here."

"Well, if so, we won't need them and next time it will be only us."

Gunter raised his arm to signal the others and got into the lead Suburban. The other drivers were already in their vehicles, except for Doug Strout who held the front passenger door to Ben's Jag open for Angel Piscara before getting into the next Suburban with Bruce and Jeannette. Each of the vehicles behind the Jag flashed their lights, and Button, in the last SUV, pulled from the curb to block oncoming traffic. Gunter started rolling slowly at first, allowing the other vehicles to fall in line.

THE DRIVE OUT through Cambridge and Belmont and into Lexington was uneventful. Gunter would drive ahead to check out any intersection and block the road at traffic lights so that the convoy didn't have to stop. They arrived at Angel Piscara's house in almost fifteen minutes less time than it usually took.

As usual, Ben parked on the shoulder of Common Street across from the Dean's house. The Dean got out and stood in the headlights, looking to make sure that no traffic was coming. Seeing none, he crossed the street. As he headed down the driveway to his house, a voice over the radio—Gunter's—crackled. "Car." Then a moment later, "State trooper. Probably headed home from a detail."

As the cruiser passed Piscara's house, his headlights flashed on two men in the driveway. One was Piscara. Ben heard a beep and static on the radio, followed by Button's voice from the last Suburban.

"We have traffic. Maybe bogeys."

The radio crackled again. This time it was Strout. "We've got company and they came loaded." Strout's hoarse voice was curt—his command voice—and Ben could hear the thunder of powerful engines in the background.

Ben jumped from the Jag. He was halfway across the street when he heard a crash. It was followed by the deep throaty rumble of a huge diesel engine. Then, another crash, this one louder than the first. The night was filled with the sound of tearing of metal and the bursting of glass.. Ben had barely cleared the road when a huge twenty-two wheeled dump truck came roaring past. This was followed closely by another identical truck. Both were bearing down on Gunter's Suburban.

Ben ran down the drive to Piscara's front door. He found it closed and locked. He felt foolish ringing the doorbell with all the mayhem behind him, but he did. He saw the Dean's wife, Eda, shuffling toward the door. Suddenly he realized he had not heard a third crash. Eda opened the door before Ben had a chance to think about Gunter. "Is Angel with you?" he said.

"No, I thought that you were bringing him home."

Gunter appeared beside Ben, out of breath from having run down the drive.

"Eda," Ben said. "Please go with this man. His name is Gunter. I will explain soon."

Sirens wailed and whooped and the road at the end of the drive soon filled with police cars and fire trucks, their flashing lights piercing the dark. The ambulances arrived just as Ben pushed through the bushes beside the house and headed to the back yard. Walking along the low back fence, he spotted a rhododendron with several broken branches. He walked into the next yard and searched around the house. Piscara and Stoekl were nowhere to be seen.

WHEN BEN GOT back to Piscara's driveway, he learned from Gunter that the state trooper had been the first one hit. The state trooper had just passed Button's Suburban and had taken the brunt of the dump truck's force, deflecting the truck slightly from its path. The truck had hit Button at the driver's side taillight, pushing it off the road. Button was badly shaken but uninjured. The trooper was dead.

The next Suburban had been hit straight on, pushing it into a tree and crushing the cabin. Bruce, Jeanette and Doug Strout were all dead.

"BEN, YOU MUST come with me *now*!" Gunter grabbed Ben's arm and started to pull him toward the lead Suburban.

Ben broke free from Gunter's grip and turned to face him squarely. "Gunter, I need to stay until they cut Strout out of the Suburban. He and I have been together a long time. He..."

Bill Button came up behind Ben and pushed him toward Gunter. "Ben, go with Gunter now. Get out of here."

"But what about Piscara?"

"Piscara is fine."

"You found him?"

"No. We don't exactly know where he is."

"Then how is he fine? You saw this guy Stoekl grab him."

"Stoekl is Treasury."

"You knew?"

"Yes, I knew. Sorry. I couldn't afford to tell anyone. Now go. This is still a live situation."

"What do you mean? Does Stoekl have Piscara or not? Is Stoekl really on our side?"

"Stoekl has gone dark. There will be no communications from him if he believes this is still a live situation. He'll stay dark until he believes the situation has stabilized. Dashkov and Sather are nowhere to be found. And this guy from Colombia, who now lives in Brazil, suddenly shows up, then he disappears too. There's a team of FBI, INS and Treasury agents on the way here now."

"Carlos Y? Are they looking for him, too?"

"They've been trying to get their hands on him for years. Now all they've got is you and they're trying to decide what they want to do with you."

"Bill, I can tell them what I know, but I can't get detained here. I need to be able to return to Paris." Ben paced back and forth in front of Bill as he spoke, gesturing wildly with his hands.

"Don't worry. The French government has already informed State that you have immunity. They have summoned the U. S. Ambassador to France to deliver the same message."

"What? Is this Marcel's doing?"

"Aren't you the French Consul in Boston?"

"The Honorary Consul for Art? Yes, but I'm not really a diplomat."

"It was part of our plan all along. An out if things went bad. You've got the title, Ben. It's your ticket out of here, but don't hang around here too long and give them time to change their minds."

"How long do I have?"

"Right now, they don't want to deal with you. Once the U. S. Attorney gets involved, all bets are off. She doesn't care much about diplomatic immunity. Treasury and State don't want to deal with the fallout and they don't want to be in the middle with Justice. The TV crews are setting up now. I'd say that you've got less than an hour before she shows up looking for airtime with you as the chief exhibit. You won't look good with your hands cuffed behind your back. The cameras love the 'perp walk'."

Gunter grabbed Ben's right arm. "Ben, I have the plane ready to take you back to Paris. You need to get out of here now."

Bill put his right hand on Ben's left shoulder and looked up into his eyes. "Claudine will want you home. I'll come before the week is up and let you know what's going on."

"Okay, but I want Strout taken care of right. He has an estranged daughter. Find her. I need to know that he'll be taken care of." Ben's face was no more than an inch from Button's, and Bill could see the fire in Ben's eyes.

"I'll take care of it myself." Button said, unblinking.

Ben backed off a few inches and his voice softened. "Thanks, Bill."

Ben ignored Gunter's entreaties to follow him to the Suburban and instead walked to the Jag. There wasn't a scratch on it. He got in and started the car. Gunter got into the passenger side, just as Ben slipped the car into drive. Together they headed to Hanscom Field.

"Gunter," he said. "We need to make sure that Bruce and Jeanette are taken care of, too. Charter a plane to take them home. Don't they live near Charlotte?"

"Yes, they do...did."

"Were they a couple?"

"No, not anymore. They divorced three years ago."

"Kids?"

"Not together, but Jeanette has a daughter with her new husband."

"How old?"

"Three."

"Oh."

THERE WAS NO black Suburban waiting for Ben when his plane landed at Orly. In its place stood Marcel's black Mercedes sedan. Two motorcycles sat in front of it, two more behind. Gendarmes. Their black-clad and helmeted riders stood ramrod straight beside their bikes. Stefan, Marcel's driver, opened the left rear door of the Mercedes as Ben approached. Ben entered to find the stern Gallic face of Marcel awaiting him.

"What were you playing at?" Marcel said, looking straight ahead, then turning and facing Ben as he waited for an answer. His face was noticeably red.

"Good morning, Marcel. How are you today?" Ben smiled at his father-in-law.

"You misjudged, and four people are dead—maybe more."

"Marcel, I was working with the best people. People with experience."

"You were working with Americans. You all suffer from terminal optimism."

"Under the circumstances, it's hard to argue with you, but I'm not really in the mood for a lecture."

"No."

They rode in silence for several minutes.

"Ben, I'm sorry that you lost a friend and that some of your people died. It really hit me, too. I have never really considered that this might happen to some of my people. They spend a good part of their lives serving us. We hire them to protect us and assume that God protects them. We never expect to face someone who has such a disregard for life. I insist on security to keep myself and my family safe from the annoying and the angry—not even considering the deadly. Don't you see now how important that is?"

"Marcel, I think a lot of people need security, but they don't get it. We do because we can afford it. I don't object to our being safe, at least not always, but I think it's a travesty that safety is denied to others. That's all."

"Are you quite sure that it is the Russian, Dashkov, who is behind this?"

"I don't really know, but that's what Bill and Doug think...or thought. The fact that it was centered around Piscara would make me believe that it well could be."

Saying Doug's name aloud drew a black cloud over Ben. He lowered his head to his hands and cried for the first time since leaving Piscara's house.

MARCEL SAT MOTIONLESS for a long few moments, then reached out and kneaded Ben's neck. "Have they found Piscara?" Ben heard the tremble in Marcel's voice.

"No, and I need to help. I'll spend a few days here, then I need to go back."

"You can't go back for the time being. As far as the U.S. Attorney is concerned, you are a suspect. They have arrested Bill Button and they have asked the French government to extradite Gunter. They want to question you too, but they have been turned down—for now."

"Shit, they arrested Bill? He's my one asset on the ground."

"Ben, don't do anything foolish. Be patient. You have responsibilities here."

"I know, Marcel. I'll agree not to return, for now. It's hard though. It hurts. I need to be here for Claudine. I need to spend time with the children. I need to pay attention to the work that Josh and his team are doing and I need to pay attention to the work of Satart Holt. But I owe so much to Piscara, and this tragedy has renewed my will to fight Sather's plans for the BIA. It's all so overwhelming and I'm so tired already." He laid back hard against the seat, his neck pressing against the head rest, his eyes closed. A deep sigh escaped from his chest.

"I'm available for you, Ben, but all of this you must do. When you come out the other side you will be stronger for it."

"Thank you, Marcel."

"For being available? You knew I would be."

"No. Well, yes. No, I meant for saying 'when' I come out the other side, not 'if'."

"*De rien.* Ah, here we are."

The car pulled to the curb in front of 11 rue Sebastien Bottin.

"Are you coming in?"

"No, I spent most of yesterday there. Give my love to everyone."

"I will. Thanks for the ride."

"Oh, by the way, I really like your new girl, Annie."

ROBERT WAS UNCHARACTERISTICALLY demonstrative in greeting Ben, and Ben thought it might have been the first time that he had seen Babette in the foyer. She kissed him twice and held him to her like a long lost son.

"But we are taking all of your time," Babette said. "And you must spend time with Claudine and the children. They are all in the garden waiting for you. Go. I will make you your tartine and allongé. Robert will bring it out to you."

"No. I want you and Robert to be in the garden with us. I have something to say."

"I will make you your tartine and allongé first; then I will come."

Ben smiled. He knew it was futile to argue with Babette when it came to tartine and allongé. It was a ritual that she needed to provide and that Ben was loathe to deny her now.

When he entered the garden, Pascha and Emma swarmed him. Abeille seemed alarmed by the commotion and crinkled up her face as if to cry, then saw Ben and reached her small arms to him. As he bent to pick her up, he saw Claudine and Annie sitting in the pergola. They stood as he approached. Claudine wobbled on her feet. Ben was able to reach out and catch her. He held her in his arms, Abeille sandwiched happily between them.

"I'm home, my love, and I'm staying home."

"For now, perhaps."

"For as long as I can and for as long as you want me."

"Let's see how much of you I can take."

Ben held her tight and took in her essence. There was a small change, barely perceptible, but it was there and it worried him. He looked to Annie and saw tears welling in her eyes. He wondered what she might know about this change in Claudine.

52

B EN ASKED ROBERT TO GATHER ALL OF THE FAMILY
and staff in the dining room. When they were ready, Ben walked
in with Claudine leaning on his arm. He sat her in a chair at the end of
the table and stood beside her.

"I want you all to know what happened in Lexington. Most impor-
tantly, I want you to know that I lost a good friend, and as a family we
lost two good people who had taken care of us. Somewhere near Boston,
a family lost a husband and a father. I have reason to believe that my
dear friend, Angel Piscara, is alive and safe, but we do not know where
he is. We will be adding some additional security here. I doubt that
there is any real danger, but we need to be safe. Annie, that means that
you will be driven home each night. If the situation warrants, you may
need to stay here. Babette, you will have an escort when you go to the
market. Robert, you will have support from two of Gunter's men. You
will all see some Gendarmes with automatic weapons posted around
the neighborhood."

"Ben, how long do you think we will need these extraordinary
measures?" Robert was standing behind Babette at the far end of the
table. He rose to his full height as he spoke.

Robert was being, Ben thought, true to form, masking any concern
behind his Gallic reserve. "I'm hoping for no more than a few days, but
it could be a couple of weeks until they find Dashkov and Piscara. I

doubt it will be longer, but I don't really know. Claudine, can you work from here for now?"

"I'm sure I can, but not more than two weeks." She turned her face up towards Ben, then looked back down at the table realizing she might have to be away from her *atelier* for a longer time. Ben knew that he was asking a lot, especially with her illness closing in on her. He would have to find a way to accommodate her.

"Thank you. Thank you all for listening. I've not told you all the details. I'm not sure how much you want to know. I'll try to answer any questions you have honestly. If you want to talk, please ask me individually and we'll find time."

53

A S ANNIE WAS LEAVING THE DINING ROOM, BEN
approached her. "Annie, I'm glad that you're here. I hope
it's not too much."

"No. It's good. You have a beautiful family." She smiled, but there
was a tic at the end that seemed a bit sad.

"Thank you. I have to tell you that I noticed the tears in your eyes
when we were in the courtyard with Claudine. Is there anything that I
ought to know?"

"Like what?"

"Is there anything happening with Claudine that I ought to know
about?"

"I don't think so. She has some balance problems, but you already
know that, according to Doctor Deschamps."

"Mizz Deschamps."

"Oh, I think she's a doctor."

"She is, but we don't address them as 'Doctor' here."

"Oh, I'm sorry. I thought that it odd that Robert called her
'Madame'."

"No reason to be sorry. I just want you to be comfortable here.
Claudine likes you very much, as does Marcel."

"I was worried that you might be uncomfortable with me here."

"I have to admit that I thought I might be. It is a bit strange, I
suppose, but I have to admit that I feel comfortable around you."

"I'm sorry about the way things happened. They weren't supposed to turn out that way."

"Perhaps they were, but we just didn't know it." Ben's smile was touched with tenderness. It was meant to make Annie feel better, but it did quite the opposite.

54

WHEN BEN ARRIVED AT THE FONDATION BERNADINE Aubrey office early the next morning, the young guard refused to let him in.

"But I'm here for a meeting with Josh Spencer."

"You are not on the visitor list, Sir."

"Because I'm not a visitor..."

"So why don't you use your staff badge?"

"Because I don't have a staff badge."

"And why don't you have a staff badge?"

"Because I'm not staff, you see..."

"I think that we're going in circles here, Sir."

Before Ben could pursue the matter, Josh walked through the front door with Diane on his arm. She ran up to Ben and kissed him softly on the lips, but was disappointed when Ben didn't blush. Ben reached his hand out to Josh.

Josh made a display of adjusting his tie and clearing his throat, but he couldn't hide his flushed face. When he noticed Ben's hand he awkwardly recovered and said, "I'm glad you're here Ben, and in one piece. We've heard the news reports. Pretty awful stuff."

"Yes, but I'm here now. I'm excited to hear about the work and your progress. I've been reading your reports, of course, but I suspect that there's more than you're writing."

"Let's go up. Have you signed in?"

Ben said, "Okay, let's get this straight once and for all. Young man, come over here." He looked at the guard's badge. "Gilles, Josh, Diane and anyone within earshot including you in the guard room, I am Ben Holt. I am the founder of this lab and the chair of the Board. I do not have a badge, I will never have a badge and I do not sign in. Am I clear?"

Gilles answered first. "Yes, Sir."

Josh raised his index finger and said, "But Ben..."

Diane grabbed his hand and lowered it to his side. "Right, no sign in."

As Ben and Josh walked though the lobby toward the elevators, Diane walked out the front door to the street. Gilles' radio crackled and a voice from the guard room filled the lobby. "I'll bet he doesn't do a time card either."

Ben turned toward Gilles, smiled a big smile, shook his head and entered the waiting elevator cab with Josh already inside pressing the door-open button.

THE PROGRESS REPORT that Josh and the research staff presented indicated substantial progress on a large number of technical issues related to a new focused beam machine designed to deliver precise and powerful radiation to a tiny spot on a tumor. The successes included refining the radiation beam focus and energy levels and reducing the size of the generator. There was still substantial work to be done on the delivery methodology and Ben urged the team to develop a delivery method that eliminated the frame that the team said was necessary to stabilize the patient's body.

"It feels more like entrapment than stabilization," Ben said.

One of the male researchers said, "That's a nice concept, but it will take years to perfect. You don't have years. This method is good enough."

Ben peered over the top of his reading glasses at the researcher. "That's no reason to stop working on a better, more elegant delivery methodology. Remember that we are dealing with people, not bodies. What if we were able to tell the tumor exactly where the tumor is? What if we developed a plan, or a map, for the computer? What if it was in 3D?"

"We're radiologists, not robotics engineers. We're not welding cars in Japan. And we're not cartographers."

"Maybe we should be."

AFTER THE REST of the team left, Josh sat down next to Ben. "You need to take it a bit easier on them. We've made extraordinary progress developing the generator and focusing the beam. If you want this to be ready for Claudine, they must maintain their focus.

"Okay. I'll give you that. I'll write a note to them thanking them for their work."

"Thank you."

"But I want you all to remember that this is the beginning, not the end. We can create something truly wonderful."

"Won't it be wonderful enough if we are to cure Claudine, or at least give her more time?" Ben arched his eyebrows, punctuating the question.

"Yes, of course it would be wonderful, but that is not enough. Great things can happen by crossing discipline lines—not being constricted by them. I won't disturb their focus, but I will be looking to create something that they never allowed themselves to dream. You asked whether it would be 'wonderful enough' if we could cure Claudine. I ask you what great mind, what great company, has a motto 'wonderful enough'? I want our motto to be one word, 'wonderful'."

"Spoken like an architect."

"Yes, of course."

55

EN LOOKED FORWARD TO HIS NEW DAILY REGIMEN
B with renewed energy. The office reorganization had lifted the
chains of management that had enslaved him and the prosecutor-forced
exile meant that he would be spending all of his time in Paris, close to
Claudine and the children. If he thought he was free of the burden of
the BIA/Piscara/Sather debacle, however, he would have been wrong.

There were negotiations between the U.S. Attorney in Boston
and the French government, with the U. S. Embassy in Paris and the
Treasury Department supporting Ben's case against deposing him.
Marcel's office in Washington was lobbying the U. S. Attorney General
to take Carmen Ortega off the case. There was so much pressure being
applied to Ortega that Ben felt some sympathy for her.

Satart Holt was experiencing a surge in new project inquiries, and
that brought new work to the boards. Marcel had asked Ben to look at
a group of abandoned Paris Metro stations spread throughout the city,
including one near the Eiffel Tower. A development group retained
Satart Holt to design the renovations and rebuilding of a former hospital along the left bank of the Seine. A wealthy entrepreneur from New
York commissioned a museum to be built in Middlebury, Vermont to
house artwork that he had collected, and another wealthy investor from
Miami commissioned the firm to design a museum to house the ex-
tensive car collection he had purchased over several years with money
realized from the sale of a family-owned chain of hospitals. For Ben, the

most intriguing project was one that grew out of his design for Ocean Park.

The as-yet-unnamed project sat along the Saugus River west of Ocean Park. It was formerly the site of General Electric's River Works plant, which still had a presence on the site. The project would be more than twice the size of Ocean Park and would be connected via a long park that would stretch several miles to cities and towns west of the site. This would be a canvas on which Ben planned to paint a lifetime of ideas on architecture, urban planning and landscape design.

BEN QUICKLY SETTLED into a daily schedule that included five hours of work each morning on Satart Holt projects. At 12:30 he would have lunch with a few key office staff at the café that had been Pascal and Ben's favorite. By 1:30 he was having a phone meeting with Bill Button, a Treasury agent named Simon Pierce and occasionally others who were working the Piscara disappearance. Bill had been released from custody within hours after his arrest. Progress was measured in very small steps, but little-by-little, pictures of the major players and their personalities started to emerge.

John Stoekl was a favorite of the Treasury Secretary, but not of his immediate managers, nor their superiors. He had spent years undercover and had developed an independence that didn't sit well with the procedure-bound. Stoekl and Button had worked together years before on a CIA-Treasury joint operation that Bill refused to talk about. He steadfastly vouched for Stoekl. When Ben asked Button why he wasn't aware of Stoekl's role in the Dashkov/Sather affair earlier, Button just shrugged. When Ben pushed him further he said, "I didn't want to believe that Dashkov flipped him, but it happens."

Dashkov had been a small-time hood and enforcer for the Russian mob. He had grabbed an opportunity to play on a bigger field when the Soviet Union collapsed. He had become wealthy because of his mob connections, but those same connections still saw him as no more than the foot soldier he had always been. They kept him out of the most lucrative deals. The Boston real estate play was to be his redemption and his revenge. He had already attracted substantial investments from the cronies who had shunned him but who were now clamoring to be let into a scheme that would move some of their more ill gotten money into the United States and launder it at the same time. A failure or long delay in the deal could be fatal for Dashkov.

Mo Sather was convinced that he ruled the world, or at least his small part of it. He also believed that Boston was, in fact, the Hub of the Universe. New York was loud and boisterous but lacked Boston's finesse. All of the other cities were merely brash pretenders. The Back Bay project was more than his answer to the other cities; it was his answer to Ben. Sather was livid over Ben's success at Ocean Park and was obsessed with proving that the student he sent fleeing from Boston was nothing more than a second-rate talent being kept afloat by his father-in-law's money.

Angel Piscara was all that he appeared to be and nothing more. He didn't so much love the BIA as possess it, and it possessed him. At 96, any other man would have moved on to a quieter, less demanding life. He was the heart of the BIA. Everyone knew that, and, despite his protestations to the contrary, so did he. His one flaw, it would seem, was that he trusted no one. Not his closest friends, not Ben. His was the only pure vision and everyone would, he believed, betray that vision and fail him in the end.

Ben was determined to prove him wrong.

Two or three other players were briefly discussed, though Bill and the others could find only tenuous connections to the disappearances of Piscara, Stoekl, Dashkov and Sather.

ONE AFTERNOON IN a status meeting in the library in Ben's home, Simon Pierce announced that he wanted to add two names to the list of players to be investigated. "The first name I want to add is Carlos Y." He wrote the name on a whiteboard.

"Why would you add his name?" one of the occasional attendees asked. "He is—or was—a Colombian drug lord who has settled into a quiet and ostensibly legal life in Rio."

"Because we're picking up chatter that seems like a thinly-veiled reference to Dashkov, and because he arrived in Paris yesterday. We believe he came to see Ben."

"Do you know him, Ben?"

Ben barely looked up from the briefing papers he was reading. "We've met."

"More, please."

"He and I shared a drink at a café in Rio."

"That's it?" Pierce got no reaction from Ben. "Okay then, one more with a connection to you, Ben."

Ben held out his upright palms and wiggled his fingers, silently saying, "Bring it on."

"Bernadine Aubrey."

Ben shrugged.

WHEN THE MEETING broke up, Bill Button pulled Ben aside. "There's more to the Carlos Y story, isn't there, Ben?"

"I shared Strout's report on the murder of his son with him. The kid was a BIA student registered under a false name. He worked for Sather as an office boy. For some reason that Strout hadn't found out yet, Sather evidently thought the boy was stealing papers documenting the BIA deal and, apparently, Dashkov had him killed. Strout conclud-ed that it was unlikely Dashkov knew he was Carlos' son. Would that have made a difference?"

"I don't know. Strout probably thought it might."

"Maybe he'd have grabbed the kid to assure Carlos' silence?"

"From what we know of Y, that might not be a healthy move. What's your take on him, Ben?"

"I found him to be a very genial man. He was cautious, but open. I had the sense that he was a tiger that could leap at any time but that was content to lie sleeping in the sun."

"And you told him that Dashkov killed his son?"

"Yes."

"Okay, so I can't see why that includes him in the cast."

"No. I wouldn't think that someone with reason to hate Dashkov would do something that might effectively support him."

AS GUNTER DROVE Ben to the lab after the Piscara team meeting, Ben knew it would be a short time before he would have to mention that Bernadine's name had come up. No one had actually seen her, or heard her voice, but there were "effects" in the Dashkov operation that pointed to her or someone deftly copying her methods. Ben also knew that if it was likely she was somehow involved, he would probably pass that information on to Daniel. He wasn't sure that he wanted Daniel involved in what could be a dangerous chase, but he was sure that Daniel would have to be told.

56

"**B**EN!"

"Josh!" Ben mimicked Josh's exclamation, which Josh ignored. Ben removed a pile of papers and reports from a chair in front of Josh's desk, dropped them on the floor and sat down.

John continued. "You're going to like this. We've made quite the breakthrough. It was something you said."

"Okay, what was that?"

"A comment about welding cars. It got one of our younger engineers thinking. He watched several hours of welding robot video and has presented a scheme that just might work. Then we learned that there is a team in Boston doing similar work with robots. They call their system Cyberknife, and guess what?"

"Josh, I have no idea."

"They use mapping schemes to control the robot." Josh threw his arms straight up in the air.

"Can we work with them?" Ben smiled, happy that his idea had been vindicated.

"We could try, but being in the United States, they have a far more complex regulatory approval process and you probably don't have that much time."

"How long before we could be ready for human testing?"

"We could possibly have a workable system within six months, but it is likely to be three to five years before it's ready for use in humans."

"And then?"

"Five to ten years for final approval, maybe more, probably not less."

Ben's heart sank. "Let's keep going. It's not likely to be available to save Claudine, but it's important work. Don't let up, even if it's not ready when..." Ben paused for a long moment, taking a deep breath. "Josh, your work may save someone else's life. Good work. It's very important."

"Ben, I have no words..."

"I know. No words, only the work."

BEN DECIDED TO walk home along the river. As usual, Gunter followed. He wanted to stop the SUV and let Ben walk home alone. He didn't know what had happened in the lab, but he sensed a change in Ben when he emerged from the building. Whatever it was had thrown a dark shroud over Ben. Gunter had always relied on his ability to read people. It had kept him alive in many tense situations. What he read in Ben was a profound sorrow and crushing isolation. This was not the Ben he knew and he hoped that he was wrong.

ROBERT WAS WAITING as Ben came through the front door into the foyer. "Sir, there is a call for you from Monsieur Winston."

"Thank you, Robert." Ben went into the library and lifted the receiver. "Hello, Blair."

"Hello, Ben, how are you?"

"Still breathing."

"That doesn't sound very good. Is everything okay?"

"Hard day, that's all."

"Well, I'm not sure that I'm going to make it any easier."

"What's up, Blair?"

"The U. S. Attorney is still pressing to interview you and has filed for extradition."

"The French government has flatly refused her."

"Yes, but she's still pressing. Her bosses have told her to back off, but she's playing on public opinion. I don't think the extradition motion will go anywhere, but she's hamming it up for the press."

"Political ambitions?" Ben asked.

"You can bet on it."

"I would bet that you have a compromise proposal."

"I do. I want to offer her an interview with you in Paris. She'll probably send an assistant. She doesn't want to make you look too important."

"Where and when?"

"You're okay with it, then?"

"Maybe. I want to know what the deal will be and I won't expose myself to their jurisdiction."

"So, you've already thought about this?" Winston was clearly not surprised.

"I have."

"Where were you thinking?"

"The Elyseés Palace."

"Really?"

"Really." Ben smiled, knowing he had taken Winston by surprise.

"Is that possible?"

"I don't know. Perhaps not. That would be my choice though. And I'm sure the Foreign Office would insist that she show up personally."

"Ben, why don't I call Marcel and check on it."

"No, I'll call Marcel. He'll call you. Whenever he tells you to arrange it is my decision, too."

"Okay, I'll let you know what happens."

"Blair, what would you think the timing would be?"

"Normally, I'd say that the negotiations would drag on for weeks, but I think I could set this up in the next few days, if the Foreign Office agrees."

"Okay, let's do it."

"You know, you already sound better."

"Hmmm. Well, it's not better and it's not likely to ever be better."

"I'm sorry."

"Goodbye, Blair."

WHEN BEN LEFT the library he almost knocked Annie over. "I'm sorry, Annie."

"I won't pretend to be." Annie surveyed Ben's face, looking for a blush or some sign that he understood her flirt. There was nothing.

"I wasn't looking."

"No, you seem preoccupied."

"Long day, tough day," Ben said, sighing.

"Well, if it makes you feel any better, Claudine had a good day. We went to her atelier and she showed me around. She took her latest sketches and talked to some of her people about the spring show."

"I didn't know she was sketching. That's great."

"I don't think she wanted you to know until she felt they were right. She's still having problems with the sight in her right eye."

"Yes, I know. That's great," Ben grimaced and paused to rethink his response, "…about the sketches, I mean. I'm so proud of her."

"Have you told her that?" Annie asked, tilting her head.

"No. Not in a long time. She thinks that my expressing pride in her work is demeaning because it assumes she is better than I thought she would be."

"Well, Ben, maybe it's time to try again."

"Why would it be different?"

"Because her work is better than she thought it would be."

"Thank you, Annie."

As Ben climbed the stairs to Claudine, Annie smiled. It felt good to be part of Ben's life again. She watched him ascend, noticing his strong shoulders and his trim butt. She remembered that she had always loved that butt. She wanted to squeeze it again. The thought shocked her and she worried that one day she might squeeze it by mistake. She went to the kitchen to make a cup of tea and calm herself before going back upstairs to give Claudine her medicine.

57

"WHY ARE YOU KEEPING ME HERE?" PISCARA DE-manded, looking up from the cup of coffee that sat before him on the dining room table.

"To save your life, sir. There are those who would prefer you were dead." Stoekl started to make a gun out of his fist, but rethought the gesture.

"Is that what all the noise was about yesterday?" Piscara didn't look up from his plate.

"It was two days ago, but, yes, it was."

"What happened to yesterday?" Piscara was now looking into Stoekl's eyes, interrogating him.

"You sat in a chair and didn't move. I had to keep checking to see if you were still alive."

"Does Eda know that I'm here, that I'm alright?"

"No, but she is safe. She has more security that anyone but the President."

"She might be worried about me." Piscara looked down into his plate again.

"For now we want everyone to be worried about you. That is what is keeping you alive." Stoekl stood in front of Piscara, his hands on his hips.

"Why me?"

"You are in the way of a plan by Anton Dashkov and Morris Sather to develop the parcel adjacent to the BIA."

"Parcel 13? I knew that Sather was up to no good. He is an evil man."

"He's a Girl Scout compared to Dashkov."

"Does Holt know about Dashkov and Sather?" Piscara asked.

"Probably most of the story. He and his people were trying to protect you. I think it was Holt who came up with the name of the operation, 'Saving Angel. ' I take it that you are "Angel'."

"Only to Eda."

"What should I call you?"

"Dean...or Dean Piscara. You choose."

"Okay, Dean. Is that your first name now?"

"It has been for many years. I was born Arcangelo Piscara." The dean puffed his chest and looked straight ahead as if looking for someone who wasn't there.

"Rather a big name to live up to."

"Dean is a bigger name to live up to."

"Hmmm. I suppose so."

"What's your name?"

"Stoekl."

"Just Stoekl?"

"Just Stoekl."

"Is that your first name now?"

"I was born Marion Stoekl."

"Ah, I see. Good choice going with 'Just Stoekl." He delivered this like an assessment of a good design decision by one of his students. No smile, just a fact.

"My friends used to call me 'John'."

STOEKL TOOK A carton of eggs, some cheese and a bag of broccoli from the refrigerator and a tomato from a bowl on the kitchen counter. He proceeded to make a large omelet. After it was cooked, he cut it in two in the pan, sliding each half onto separate plates. He took half a baguette, cut it into narrow slices and set half of the slices on each plate. He took one plate to Piscara and kept the other for himself.

"Do you make Bolognese?"

"I have. Many times. My mother was Italian."

"From where?"

"Brooklyn. But her family was from Emilia-Romagna."

"Will you make me Bolognese?"

"When we get out of here I'll make you the best Bolognese you've ever had."

"I doubt that. My mother was Italian too."

"Yes."

"When will we be leaving here?" Piscara pleaded now.

"I don't know."

"Why?"

"It's complicated. We still don't know where Dashkov is. We think that Dashkov has a mole deep within 'Operation Saving Angel'."

"That's not good news."

"No."

"I don't like 'Saving Angel.' It makes me miss Eda."

"I know it must be hard, but it's necessary. I'm the only one who knows where you are. If anyone else knew, we could both be dead."

"Why do you do this, Just Stoekl?"

"What do you mean?"

"Do you do it to be a hero? Do you do it for the money? Are you a fantastical character?"

"It's my job. I work for Treasury."

"Treasury?"

"The United States Department of the Treasury. I'm a Special Agent. I investigate international money laundering schemes and try to close them down."

"You don't look like that guy. You look like a thug."

Stoekl was surprised by Piscara's comment, but, looking into the older man's eyes, saw no malice there. He realized that, if Piscara had filters once, they were long gone. "That helps me in my work. I work undercover. But I have a degree from the London School of Economics and a doctorate in International Finance from HBS and the Kennedy School."

"So you're Doctor Stoekl. Where did you do your undergraduate work?"

"Harvard."

"Ah, a Harvard boy."

"Yes, sir."

"We often say that it takes us three years to take the Harvard out of our architecture professors and turn them into real teachers."

"In my job, we don't get three years."

58

BEN'S INTERVIEW WITH CARMEN ORTEGA, U. S. Attorney for Boston, was arranged to be held in the Salon Bleu of the Elyseés Palace. There were to be five people present: Ortega; her First Assistant, Frank Leahy; Blair Winston; a criminal defense attorney from Winston's office, Tim Morris; and Ben.

A senior officer from the French DCRI, the Central Directorate of Interior Intelligence, greeted the Americans and scanned each with a hand-held metal detector.

"Aren't you going to scan him?" Ortega gestured toward Ben.

"Monsieur Holt is a French diplomat and citizen." The DRCI officer sniffed. He was clearly unimpressed by Ortega.

"That is prejudicial and immediately colors these proceedings."

"Attorney Ortega, this is not a 'proceeding.' It is a courtesy interview. We have made that clear to your office." Tim Morris spoke without anger, but firmly.

Ben recognized Morris' intent to control the tenor of the proceedings and that he was happy Ortega had given him the opportunity to set the tone from the beginning.

MORRIS HAD ARRANGED the seating at the long dark table so that Ortega and Leahy were seated facing the tall windows that overlooked the courtyard. He had asked to have the heavy drapes removed so that only the nearly transparent curtains remained. The result was that the two American prosecutors faced a bright masking light and the distracting movements in the courtyard.

"I hope you don't mind that we have brought a voice recorder so that we can recall our interview later." Ortega placed an emphasis on the word, 'interview.'

"We will be recording the interview, as well," Winston said. He made no move to place a recorder on the table and Ben could see a question arising in Ortega's eyes, but she didn't speak.

"Shall we start?" Ortega flipped over several pages of a yellow legal pad, flipped a few back, then found the page she wanted. "Mister Holt, can you give us your name and address for the record?"

Morris spoke. "Miss Ortega, that sounds like a deposition question. This is not a deposition."

"Let me rephrase that. Ben, where do you live?"

Ben looked to Winston, who nodded.

"We have homes in Paris, Cannes, Saint Barth's, New York, Boston, Woodstock Vermont, Nantucket and Washington DC. Actually one in Boston and one in Lynn."

"That's quite a list. Where do you consider your home to be?"

"Paris."

"Are you a French citizen?"

"Yes."

"You're not a U. S. citizen?"

"I have dual citizenship."

"You are the French consul in Boston?"

"I am an Honorary Consul for the Arts to the United States."

"What are your duties?"

Blair Winston intercepted the question. "Mister Holt is the face of the French government on issues relative to the arts. He helps to foster and support the activities of French arts and artists in the United States."

"And what does your typical day as the face of the French government look like?"

"There is no 'typical' day. For the most part, I attend openings and other events that are showing the works of French artists and I help organizations that want to show French works of art make contacts in both the United States and France."

"Are you authorized to approve visas or assist with passport problems?"

Ben conferred in a whisper with Blair Winston. "I understand that I am."

"Have you ever done so?"

"No."

"So you primarily attend a lot of parties."

"A few well-chosen ones."

"Are you too busy with other business to attend official events?"

"Not particularly."

"Well then, why don't you attend more events? I would assume that's a central part of the job."

"I get bored."

'Does your wife attend events with you?"

"No."

"Why not? Isn't that part of being a diplomat's wife?"

"She's dying." Ben stared into Ortega's eyes and saw the discomfort there. He watched her scribble a note on a small pad and slip it to Leahy, who read it and shrugged.

Ortega sat silently for a long couple of minutes, then got up and walked to a side table where she filled a glass with water. She stood by the side table and drank slowly from the glass. Leahy took over the questioning.

"What is your relationship with Arcangelo Piscara?"

"Angel Piscara is—or was—a mentor and a close friend."

"Why do you say 'was'? Is he dead?"

"He was once my mentor and he saved my life. As time has gone on, our roles have changed. That's just a part of life."

"Do you know that he is dead?"

Morris intervened. "Unless you have information that we are not aware of, I'd suggest that you meant 'Do you think that he is dead?'"

"As you wish." Leahy raised his hands in front of him and flipped the palms open in a gesture of frustration.

"Is that your question?" Morris asked.

"Not really." Leahy stared at Ben.

"Then I suggest that we move on. Mister Holt will not be part of a fishing expedition."

Ortega returned to the table. "Ben, do you think that Piscara is dead?"

"I don't know. I didn't think so in the beginning, but it has been a long time since we've heard anything from him or from Stoekl."

"What is your relationship with Stoekl?"

"None."

"What do you know of him?"

"Apparently, nothing. We thought he was a bad guy, but it turned out he is a good guy—or so I'm told."

Ben could tell from Ortega's reaction shat she knew even less about Stoekl than Ben did.

"What is your relationship with Bill Button?"

"I suppose we're friends, close acquaintances anyway. It's hard to really know someone like Button. There's always something hidden, something left unsaid. And yet, I trust him as much as anyone I know."

"Why?"

"I don't really know. Perhaps because he has never given me a solid reason not to."

"Strout?"

"Doug Strout? I loved him. He knew things most men never know. Sometimes dark things, but he was never dark, he was the most optimistic guy I know. What he didn't know he could quickly find out. I trusted him with my life. I doubt that I could ever trust anyone the way I trusted him. He was a gem of a man."

"Gunter Steuben?"

"My head of security. Worked for my father-in-law. Keeps my family safe. Very competent. He is family."

"Bernadine Aubrey?"

"My mother-in-law. We thought she was dead, but her name came up recently."

"In what regard?"

"In some connection to this situation. I'm not sure what the connection is or was. Her name came up once."

"Is there a connection between Piscara's disappearance and your son Daniel's search for Missus Aubrey?"

"God, no. He has been trying to follow her trail for a while."

"Aren't you worried about his safety?" Ortega tilted her head and looked concerned.

"Every day, but he's an adult and he controls his own life. Besides, I doubt she'd hurt her oldest grandson."

"But others might?"

"Yes."

"Mister Dashkov?"

"I don't know him at all."

"Morris Owen Sather?"

"One of the true assholes of the world. Entirely without scruples and wholly self-serving. But he's a coward. I don't see him as capable of actually hurting Piscara."

"Carlos Y."

"Met him once. No, twice. I've had a few dealings with him at a distance. He's closer to my business partner."

"And he's a killer."

"So I've heard. He was always a perfect gentleman with me."

"Is that why you passed on to him a CIA report identifying Dashkov as the party who ordered the murder of his son?"

"Morris interjected. "Miss Ortega, Mister Holt will not answer that question."

"Of course not. Mister Holt, one more name: Simon Pierce."

"He's one of you. Justice or Treasury, I mean. Justice and Treasury Joint Task Force."

"Yes. Are you aware of the purpose of the Task Force?"

"Generally, yes. They are investigating and trying to dismantle a network that finances terrorism and organized crime internationally."

"And why would you be privy to that confidential information?"

Leahy came back to life. "We have been kept in the dark about that. By our own people."

Ortega glared at him.

Ben smiled. "Perhaps because I'm the French consul. Diplomacy and all that."

"We're done here." Ortega started to slide a sheaf of papers into a brown briefcase.

"I have one question for you. Why did you ask me about Pierce?"

It was Ortega's turn to smile. "I guess they don't tell you everything."

BEN WISHED HE could call Doug Strout. He wanted to know more about Pierce before they met again. He called a familiar number.

"Bill, we need to talk about Pierce."

59

"WE'VE BEEN HERE MORE THAN A WEEK. WHEN can I go home?" Piscara had stopped his back and forth pacing to ask his question.

"Dean, this is our seventh day. Why don't you watch some TV and calm down."

"I don't watch TV." Piscara collapsed onto a sofa, pouting.

"I have some movies for you, all in the original Italian." Stoekl cocked his head and smiled at Piscara, much as he might try to engage a child.

"Maybe later. Maybe I'll read." Piscara got up slowly from the sofa, using his arms to help him stand. He moved to a club chair that sat under a floor lamp.

"Good idea."

"Tell me, how well do you know Holt?" Piscara asked, as he opened a book.

"Never met him."

"You might like him. Tough kid, but gentle on the outside. Somewhat the opposite of you."

"Maybe I'm tough on both sides." Stoekl smiled and beat on his chest mimicking the Tarzan character.

"No."

"He sounds like a good guy." Stoekl crouched in front of Piscara, addressing him at eye level.

"He is. He's really quite special. When everyone else is creating heat, he calmly and confidently creates light. I think you'd like him."

"I have worked with a guy who is close to him."

"Who is that, Just Stoekl?" Stoekl thought that he might have caught a flash of smile from Piscara.

"Bill Button."

"Yes, I've met Button several times. Holt knows him. I can't say that I know him though. Seems like a hard guy to know."

"Occupational hazard."

BEN'S NEW DRIVER, Bet—the name she preferred to her given name, Bethanie—handed Ben a note just as she opened the SUV's door for him. He unfolded the single fold with one hand and the words he read chilled him.

"Ben. Come home immediately. Annie."

WHEN BEN WALKED into the foyer, the house was strangely, absolutely silent. More than silent. All sound seemed to have been sucked out of the space. He stood at the foot of the stairs for a moment and took a deep breath. As he prepared to take the first step, Robert appeared from the back of the house, followed by Annie and, behind her only half a step, Babette.

Robert took Ben's jacket and stepped aside for Annie. "We had a bad day, but she's resting now. The doctor just left."

"What happened?"

"She collapsed at the top of the stairs and lost control of all functions, all control in her body."

"Did she faint or pass out?'

"No. She was fully aware, fully present."

"What did Isabel say?"

"Doctor Deschamps thinks the tumor is growing and that it is pressing on the area of her brain that handles muscle control. She wants Claudine to have some tests tomorrow."

"Thank you, Annie. I'll go see her now."

"I'll come with you." Annie reached for Ben's arm but missed.

"I'll go see her alone first. I'll call if I need you."

"Okay."

Babette stepped forward with a small tureen in her hands, wrapped in a white linen towel. "I've some onion soup for her. She hasn't eaten. It's no wonder she fainted."

"Babette!" Robert barked.

Ben tensed and looked at Robert, surprised by his out of character outburst. He turned back to Babette.

"Thank you, Babette." Ben took the tureen gently.

"Sir, I'll take that up for you." Robert reached for the tureen.

"No, Robert, I'll take it up. Thank you."

Robert rocked back on his heels.

Ben turned to the room, paused for a long moment, then smiled and spoke. "Listen, the three of you. I really appreciate all you do and all you have done for us. Robert and Babette, I love you both. Claudine has always set the rules for how this house is run. You have, except for some clandestine accommodations to me, always run by those rules. The time for rules is over. Now it is time to just love each other, and that will be our only rule. Now, I'm going to go love my wife and bring her some of Babette's wonderful soup."

"There are two spoons," Babette chirped.

"We will share one." Ben handed Babette the second spoon and ascended the stairs. He didn't notice the tears filling the eyes of Babette and Annie, or the quick flick of Robert's hand across his cheek.

"WHAT DRAMA HAVE you created now, Claudine?"

"Come sit with me, Ben." Claudine looked tired and wan, her face thin. She was sitting with several pillows supporting her back.

"I will. Let me drag this table over and we will share Babette's soup."

"I'm not hungry."

"I know, but you will eat just a little."

"Ben. Please sit. We need to talk about how I want to die."

""We will, but first a spoonful of soup." Ben's voice was calm, and he was surprised that his heart was calm, too. He sat on the bed with the soup on a small table pulled close to him. He dipped the spoon into the soup, drawing it toward him. He raised the spoon and took a tiny sip before offering it to Claudine. She sipped almost silently to take the broth. When Ben lifted the handle of the spoon, the thin strands of onion slipped onto Claudine's bare neck. Claudine closed her eyes, embarrassed. Ben leaned over and sucked the onions from her neck. Claudine laughed and Ben laughed with her.

"It's great to hear you laugh," he said.

"I'm not sure I like it. You know I'm not a laugher. What is happening to me?"

"I don't know, but I know you're not going to die—not yet."

"But I want to talk about it, Ben."

"And we will, right now."

"Are you sure you are ready, Ben?"

"I'm sure I will never be ready, but you are, and I want to hear you."

"Okay."

"Okay, then."

"First, I want you to know I love you. I may not always be the most warm, the most expressive lover. I don't believe in that. I find it phony and my love for you is very real."

"I know."

"And I love the children. They must see me as the tough headmistress and you as their co-conspirator against the old hag's rules, but I love them dearly."

"They know."

"So here are my rules: I don't want to be drugged; I don't want to be a vegetable lying on this bed; when the time comes I will need your help…"

IT WAS ALMOST an hour and a half before Claudine fell into a quiet sleep. Ben sat for a while, watching her breathe and counting to test the even-ness of intervals between each breath. Then he went downstairs with the empty tureen and found Annie and Babette in the kitchen.

"She's sleeping quietly now. We finished the soup. Thank you, Babette."

"Can I make you some dinner? That soup was not enough for you."

"No. Thank you, Babette. I'm going to go over to the Foundation and read for a while."

"But it's after twenty-two hours."

"I know the time. It's not something we have a lot of."

"Let me make a baguette and ham to take with you."

"Okay. And some cornichons."

Babette smiled and hummed a light tune as she worked. Ben went out into the foyer with Annie.

"She—Claudine—should write down her wishes, her health care instructions. For legal reasons." Annie instructed Ben.

"This is France, not the United States. She has told me her rules for dying. I will respect them, but now I'm going to work so she can live."

"Does she want to live?"

"By her rules and only her rules, yes." Ben stepped to the front door, opened it and turned back to look at Annie for a moment. He nodded a good-bye. Then he went out and closed the door firmly.

BEN SPENT TWO and a half hours in his office at the foundation reading reports, most authored by Josh, detailing the successes—and the dead ends—of his research team's work. The biggest single problem seemed to be the mapping protocols. Work on the beam focus and on the safety mechanisms to be included in the robotic controls were near a level that could allow animal testing. If the accuracy of the mapping could be improved, testing could begin.

It was the final entry in the latest evaluation of Claudine that struck the blow to Ben's chest.

"Prognosis: Two to four months."

BEN FELT BESIEGED: Claudine's setback earlier in the day; Ortega's campaign to tie Ben to Piscara's abduction; the disappearance of Sather, Stoekl and Dashkov; and the reorganization of Satart Holt. He was haunted by the death of Doug Strout, half-expecting to awake from his nightmare and find him alive. At times he felt it was all a fantasy or a dream, left only to be smacked in the gut by the knowledge it was all starkly real.

BEN GOT UP from his desk and walked to the large glassed doors that separated his office from the shallow balcony that ran around the perimeter of the building at this level, just above the meeting rooms on the floor below. He sat on a bench and watched the twinkling lights that always lit up the Paris night. He heard the pop-pop wail of an ambulance pulling into the emergency court of one of the nearby hospitals and realized, as the siren died, that the phone in his office was ringing. Probably a wrong number at this hour, he thought, and he let it ring until it stopped, then, thinking it might be news about Claudine, he walked toward his desk to check the number on the display. Just as he got to his desk, the phone rang again.

He lifted the receiver. "Hello?"

"Ben, it's Severine. I have sad news. Pascal has passed."

Ben spoke slowly, knowing that Severine was reading text on a screen as he talked. He pictured her sitting before the screen and couldn't help but recall how attractive she was, how struck he had been by her beauty the day they had met in the Satart Holt Paris office. She had a long neck, like Claudine, but her black hair was longer and fell around her often-bare shoulders. Her round breasts had always been one of her unavoidable features, roaming free as they did beneath the solid white tops she wore in Rio and the black tops she wore in Paris. He found himself embarrassed to have these feelings about Severine. She was Pascal's wife, now widowed, and he had Claudine.

In answer to his questions, she told him Pascal had been sitting in the courtyard after dinner, reading. Severine had been sitting near him and watching a hot air balloon as it hovered above the park that abutted their home. She had said something about the balloon's colors to Pascal. Getting no response, she'd looked over at him and seen he had fallen asleep. She had reached over to pull up the blanket draped over his legs and had realized then he wasn't breathing. It had all been so peaceful. She had sat with him for an hour or so before summoning help.

She asked whether Ben could come to say goodbye and lead the memorial service.

"Yes, of course. Will the service be there or here?"

There was a delay as the voice-to-text device interpreted Ben's response.

"The family service will be here on Thursday. The memorial service will be at the museum. Will Claudine be able to come?"

"I'll fly in alone for the family service. Can we help organize the memorial service?"

Another delay. "Yes. That would be wonderful."

"I'll have someone contact your people tomorrow."

Another voice came on the line. "Mister Holt, this is Martha, Severine's assistant. They can call me."

"Very good, Martha. How is Severine?"

Delay. "I am well. Pascal and I shared much love. We were happy. I am happy he left us peacefully. Now, Ben, you are not telling me about Claudine. What has happened?"

"She is not well, I'm afraid. She will insist, of course, that she be at the memorial service. You must stay with us when you come."

A delay, this time longer than before.

"Ben, you will have time to be afraid later. Pascal always admired your ability to set aside your fears and attack the problem presented to you. He thought it was your yard of brick."

Ben chuckled at Severine's reference to the Brickyards where he grew up. "Yes, it was my yard of brick, but that was long ago."

BEN WALKED HOME. The omnipresent black Suburban followed. When he arrived at the house, he headed for the library. He knew what he was looking for and where it sat in the bookcase. He took down the book from its place among the leather-bound volumes and lay down on the sofa to read. He soon fell asleep with the open book splayed across his chest.

Annie often sat in the library to write her notes after seeing Claudine. When she entered that morning, she was surprised to find Ben snoring lightly on the sofa. *The Brickyard* by Kathryn Grover had fallen to the floor beside him.

THE NEXT EVENING, after a late night at Satart Holt, Ben went directly up to bed when he got home. He slipped in next to Claudine, lying on his back and watching the light play on the ceiling as the potted magnolias on the roof deck danced a waltz in the light breeze. In recent days he had been sleeping in the room next door—the bed Claudine used when his snoring kept her awake or when she had a show coming up—but now he wanted to be next to her, to not waste any of the moments they might have left.

Lying there, he devised a plan to fly to Rio early in the morning, stay with Severine for the day and attend the family service. He would leave at midnight Rio time and be back in Paris by early the next afternoon. It was the most efficient plan he could conjure as it would lose the least amount of time with Claudine, the kids and the people he needed to see in Paris.

Yes, the people he needed to see in Paris, he thought. He could call from the plane tomorrow, but one party couldn't wait. He got out of bed and went into Claudine's office. He called the Foundation's office and dialed Josh's extension.

Impatient to get past Josh's greeting, he pressed # and the phone beeped once. "I need to see you Friday at *quatorze heures*, at two o'clock. Please clear your schedule for an hour."

Ben went back to bed, pondered the ceiling for a moment, then curled his body around Claudine's. She said something he didn't understand and fell back asleep.

60

SEVERINE WAS WAITING AT THE BOTTOM OF THE ROLL-ing flight of stairs beside the plane when Ben stepped out the door. Behind her waited the ubiquitous black Suburban with an immense Asian man standing by the open rear door.

Severine leaned into Ben, hugged him and turned her cheek, right, then left, then right again, to accept Ben's kisses. She was almost exactly Ben's height. She said nothing but moved toward the Suburban, where her driver was waiting, holding the door. She entered the SUV and addressed the driver. "Thank you, Tan."

"Thank you." Ben looked closely at the driver as he passed. He was at least six foot six and within a whisper of three hundred pounds. Ben could make out the bulge of a large gun under Tan's black jacket.

Once in the Suburban, Severine explained that Tan was Samoan and that Pascal had designed a home for his parents who were quite a bit smaller than Tan, such that Tan's father was the brunt of his friends' jokes about the questionable paternity of the son. The father was an investment advisor who could give as good as he took. He claimed that while he may not know the father of his own son, he was happy to have been the father of all of his friends' sons and that—since they were all impotent—his son's father was probably a quarryman and one of his investments.

The story made Ben like Tan, and his father, instantly. He would meet Tan's father, Severine said, at the service. The father had become one of Pascal's best friends in Rio and a frequent lunch partner.

After a brief silence, talk became more serious. Severine reported that Pascal had been cremated that morning in accordance with his wishes.

"I'm sorry to hear that. I was hoping to see his face one more time."

"When we talked about the possibility he might die, and he talked about his wish to be cremated, he said that he knew you would want to see him one last time, but that I should proceed with the cremation before you arrived. He said that you would have all of the best pictures of him in your mind."

Ben thought for a moment. "He was a very wise man."

"I always thought of him as a poet. He lived his life as a poem."

Ben smiled broadly and deeply. "I never thought of that, but he did, didn't he?"

"He left you a letter."

"Have you read it?"

"No."

"Perhaps we can read it together."

"I would love that, but he forbade it."

"Well, he's not here to enforce it, so..."

"I expect that he knew you would say that. He hinted as much in his letter to me."

"Then we will not disappoint him."

"There is another letter for you at the house, one from Carlos Y."

"Good."

"Good?"

"I thought I might hear from him somehow. Frankly, I expected to hear sooner, but I know he is careful about his communications."

"He was always very talkative with Pascal and me. Then one day I realized he said nothing that revealed anything. Just talk over the fence, if you know what I mean."

"I do."

It was so nice to talk to Severine face-to-face, Ben thought. Her lip-reading was impeccable and the artifice of the text machine was no longer a barrier. "Tell me, Severine, did Pascal know about the disappearance of Dean Piscara? Did he ever talk about it?"

"He knew from the newspapers. He was quite shocked at first, but after a short while, maybe a week, he never mentioned it again. I thought it might be that he felt that he might be disloyal to you."

"Yes, he might feel that."

"Do you think that Piscara is dead?"

"No. I think that he is very much alive, but it is frustrating not knowing where he is."

"Why is he still missing?"

"We're not sure. But I'm worried that the longer he is missing, the greater the chance he is being used as a pawn in a dangerous game."

"What can you do about it?"

"That's what I'm trying to figure out. One of my best people is gone. I'm relying on a friend—who has his own agenda—and someone who we thought was one of the bad guys—who may be our good guy—and then there is an agent—who was *supposed* to be a good guy, but who may be a mole—and two bad guys, one of whom is truly nasty-bad and the other who is just a greedy, self-serving opportunist, who may be in over his head."

"My god, it sounds like a TV movie."

"Yes, but it's all too real."

"Tell me about Claudine." Severine laid her hand on Ben's knee, gently squeezing it. He noticed her long fingers and liked them on his knee. Raising his gaze back to her face, he composed himself.

"It's a battle for time. We are close to a potentially effective treatment, but we may be too late. She can't walk now and I'm worried that she may give up before we are ready to test our treatment protocol."

"Can I come back with you tonight? I'd like to be with her for a while."

"I think she'd love that."

"Then it is done."

LATER THAT AFTERNOON, Ben and Severine read Pascal's letter together. When they were done, Ben folded the letter into a paper airplane and flew it across the garden. Then they laughed and hugged. When Ben dropped his arms, Severine reached out and held his face in her hands. She kissed him softly on the lips, then blushed and turned away, brushing Ben's shoulder with her hand as she did.

Ben awkwardly excused himself and took Carlos Y's letter to a far corner of the garden. He unfolded the single small sheet of paper and read.

"Be strong, my friend. Meet me for dinner at the café at 20 hours."

BEN WAITED AT the beach-side café for nearly a half hour and there was still no sign of Carlos. As he prepared to leave, two large black-suited men at a nearby table rose and blocked his way.

"Mister Holt, Mister Y apologizes for his tardiness and asks that you please wait for him," one of the men said.

Ben sat back in his chair. Y arrived fifteen minutes later, apologizing profusely and begging forgiveness for his unforgivable absence. They talked for nearly half-an-hour about Pascal and their remembrances of him, then talked for another fifteen minutes about the arrangements for the memorial service.

Ben caught a glimpse of Y's big watch and began to excuse himself, telling Y of his plan to fly back to Paris with Severine at midnight.

"Yes, of course, you must go. I will hope to see you at Pascal's service. Please let my men guide you home. There will be terrible traffic further along the beach. It seems that a body has been found. It was horribly disfigured, but I understand they are about to identify it as belonging to a Russian named Dashkov."

Ben searched Y's eyes but found nothing more than a peaceful face. "Thank you for your kindness, Carlos—and for the guidance of your men."

They both stood and embraced.

61

WITHIN MINUTES OF REACHING CRUISING ALTI-
tude, Severine had fallen asleep. Ben watched her face for several minutes. Like Carlos Y, her face was peaceful and quiet. Ben wished
that he could share their apparent comfort, but even as he felt for them,
a huge tug from within his chest dragged him back to his own gnawing
pain. He had just lost his closest friend, he had already lost Strout and
his brother, Don, and he was struggling to keep Claudine alive. Piscara
was, he was told, safe, but no one knew where he or Stoekl was. At least
his concerns about Dashkov were over.

Ben briefly wished that it had been he who had passed away quietly in his sleep. The pain would be over and the unending pressure
gone. Then he remembered that he was still needed by Daniel and
Pascha, Emma and Abeille. Well, maybe not Daniel he thought, and
smiled. And if he passed, who would save Claudine? No, now was not
the time to go; now was the time to stand up. Whether he succeeded
or failed, he must be present to fight on. He removed Pascal's letter
from his jacket pocket and read the next to last paragraph again.

"I know that many are impressed by your designs, by their unfail-
ing elegance and sometimes by their unpredictability. For me, I have
always been taken by your quiet strength, unbent as it is by buffeting
winds and the siren lure of public praise alike."

Ben thought that some praise might feel good just now, but quickly realized that he would only consider it a tinny noise. He had work

to do. He looked to Severine, leaned over and drew up the blanket that was covering her legs and tucked it around her waist.

THE SUBURBAN HAD barely come to a stop in front of Ben's home, when Severine had opened the car door and was standing on the sidewalk. Robert was just opening the mansion's front door. She rushed up the walkway and quickly leaned over to kiss both of his cheeks before disappearing into the house.

By the time Ben had entered the foyer, Severine had raced up the stairs and Aniie was chasing up the stairs a half-dozen steps behind. "You can't just barge in here," she screamed. "This is a private residence. Stop where you are!"

Severine, of course, heard nothing.

Ben tried to call out, but he had fallen to his knees, laughing so hard that he started coughing uncontrollably.

Annie had just reached the top of the stairs when Severine turned and saw her.

"Ah, you must be Annie. I have heard so much about you from Claudine. From Ben, I get nothing, of course. Come, we must go to Claudine."

Annie heard Ben's coughing and was about to head back down to him when Severine caught her arm and pulled her along. "Leave him to Robert. Let's go see Claudine."

"Are you Severine?"

"Yes, yes. And you are Annie."

"I must say that you are not what I expected."

"Why is that?"

"I'm not sure. I had a picture of you in my mind, and you are *not* that picture."

"Well, we will have time to make new pictures. Now let's go see Claudine."

FOR THE NEXT half-hour, the house was full of laughter. It could be heard in the Library all the way from the third floor. Finally, Ben decided that he should intervene, lest Claudine get too tired and feel the effects for several days. He knew that she would insist on being at Pascal's memorial.

When he entered the bedroom that she had started to use as her sickroom during the day, he found Severine laid out in Claudine's favorite chaise with Annie sitting on its footrest. Claudine was standing beside the bed, leaning against it for support. They were sharing stories. Annie was talking now and Ben heard her late husband's name. He grimaced, realizing that he had never heard Harold's name from her lips before. It bothered him that he could easily forgive Annie for breaking his heart so many years ago, but a dead man that he hadn't met, never.

He stopped outside the bedroom door, took a deep breath, stood tall and entered the room.

"Sorry to break this up ladies, but can I have my wife for a little while? After breakfast, she is yours."

"Oh, Ben, you're not going to go to the office today, are you? You should spend the day with us."

Ben was surprised by Claudine's request. She was often—and not so secretly—pleased when he left her alone for the day. He often wondered how she filled her time with so much reading when her days had been packed to both ends with work in her studio.

"No. I will be meeting with some people here. When we are done, I will spend some time with you."

"Is it Bill?" Claudine asked.

"Yes, and some others."

"When will that be over? Eda must be beside herself."

"She would be, but Eda has Alzheimers."

"When?" Claudine's voice was very small.

"For some time, I guess. Angelo either hid her condition, or didn't know, himself."

"That's terrible." Annie shook her head slowly.

"Maybe not. She is unaware of his kidnapping. I think that the worry might have killed her."

Severine walked to the bedroom door with Ben. "If you don't mind, I'd like to stay here for a while. I think that I can help Claudine—a little, in any case."

"You are always welcome here, Severine, but before you do anything with Claudine, please talk with Annie."

"Of course. Perhaps I can help Annie, too."

"No voodoo."

"Maybe just a little magic." She kissed Ben lightly on his cheek.

62

SIMON PIERCE WAS ALREADY IN THE LIBRARY WHEN
Ben returned. As Ben reached the open door, the doorbell rang and
Robert admitted Bill Button and two men that Ben didn't recognize.

"Ben, this is Carl Blass and Jake Isaacs," Bill said. "Carl is with
Treasury, he's Pierce's immediate superior and Jake is from the FBI but
working on the joint task-force on money-laundering with Treasury."

Ben shook their hands. "Pierce is already here."

Blass asked, "Can we meet somewhere else in the house before we
go in and see Pierce?"

"Yes, of course; we can meet in the garden."

Blass walked to the open Library door, leaned in and spoke to
Pierce. "Hang in, Pierce. We'll be with you soon."

Ben and Bill looked at each other inquisitively. Ben shook his head.
"Why did you do that?"

"I didn't want him to get antsy and leave."

IN THE GARDEN, Isaacs laid out the case against Pierce. He had
become a mole for Dashkov, probably as a result of crushing gambling
debts, and might, in fact, know where Dashkov was. He could be
convinced to give up that information with the right handling.

"I know where Dashkov is." Ben was surprised that the U. S. Government hadn't gotten the news.

"You do?" Isaacs and Blass exclaimed in unison.

"He's dead. Made to look like his body washed up on a Rio beach."

"How can we confirm that?"

"How do you normally confirm that? Call the Rio Police? Ask the Embassy to get confirmation? Read the Rio newspaper?"

"I wonder if Pierce knows." Blass stroked his chin. "Let's play that angle out when we question him. I'll take the lead on it since he's my guy. Okay, shall we go see him now?"

Ben looked at Blass quizzically. "Unless he's an absolute idiot, he's not in the Library."

"Sure he is. I gave him an express order to stay." Blass turned to Isaacs and Button. "You heard me give him an express order, did you not?"

Button smirked and shook his head. Isaacs looked at the floor.

They all rose. Isaacs and Blass hurried to the Library. Ben and Button lagged behind. The Library was empty.

"Why would he do that? I gave him an express order. This will not be good for him." Blass took a small notebook from his jacket pocket and wrote a quick note.

63

BEN JOINED SEVERINE AND CLAUDINE AFTER HIS meeting and they headed for the garden. Annie brought Claudine her morning ration of pills. She stood and watched as Claudine swallowed each pill, followed by a drink of water.

"Join us, Annie." Ben stood and pulled out a chair. Babette soon appeared and served lunch. The sun was shining and the mood was mellow.

"How was your meeting?" Annie asked.

"Insane, totally and absolutely insane."

"Is that good insane, like the kids say?"

"If someone's life wasn't at stake, it would have been hilarious. As it was, it was very sad and confirms my inclination to proceed on my own,"

"Be careful Ben, they're probably nasty people." Annie reached cut and touched Ben's arm.

Ben was surprised by Annie's admonition. Perhaps, he thought, she never really knew him. He was done with procedure. It was time to get nasty.

AFTER LUNCH, BEN excused himself and went to the Library. He dialed a number he had committed to memory. "Carlos, Can you meet me in Gustavia tomorrow? I'll send my plane for you. You'll have diplomatic cover. I'm holding a conference on money-laundering and its links to terrorism."

"How many people will be there?"

"Two."

WHILE BEN AWAITED Carlos' arrival in Gustavia, he plotted a diagram in his notebook. It had five names: Piscara, Y, Button, Stoekl and himself. His name was at the center of the diagram and he connected the other names to his own with solid lines. He added Gunter and joined his name to the core group with dashed lines. He then drew a second dashed line from his name to Button and to Y and thought some more about each of these two lines. Before the day was over, he would need to decide how much trust to place in each of them. He needed at least one of them, maybe both.

Ben rose from his chair on the deck of the Bella Santé, Marcel's yacht that was docked in its homeport of Gustavia Harbor. It was the appointed time for his meeting with Carlos and he had gotten a call from his pilot reporting that Y had left the runway in the car that Ben had sent.

Within moments, Ben saw the black sedan stop at the drive-up and Carlos emerge, dressed in a crisp white shirt, tan slacks, and a beige linen jacket. He looked very relaxed and wore a bright smile.

"Carlos. So good of you to come." Ben held his hand out to greet Y at the head of the gangway.

"Your invitation was intriguing."

"I'll get right to the point: Can I trust you?"

"No."

"Okay, why can't I trust you?"

"I have no investment in your situation. My interests are my own and they are the objectives by which I invest. Am I being clear?"

"Yes, very. That is very helpful."

"What do you need?"

"I need to get to Mister Stoekl, preferably with his agreement, but, if necessary, without it."

"And why do you think that I can help you with that?"

"Because you are a resourceful man and I believe that you can point me in the right direction."

"Perhaps. Perhaps."

"How well did you know my mother-in-law?"

Y looked as if the question had taken him by surprise. "We had a fruitful business relationship."

"You trusted her."

"We have interests that align."

Ben watched Carlos' eyes, wondering if he realized the mistake that he had just made. "Shall we have lunch?"

"Of course."

BEN PICKED UP the phone next to his chair. The captain appeared in a few moments with a bottle of wine and a cooler carafe. Two young, thin, well-tanned women followed him, each carrying an iced platter. The food was from Maya's and included a ceviche and a carpaccio of fish, thin slices of raw red snapper and yellowfin tuna. There were oysters and shrimp, the local langouste, calamari and a colorful array of local vegetables. The captain poured the entire bottle of Cassis rosé into the cooler carafe and set it on the table. He disappeared for a moment and then returned with two dishes filled with wedges of bright yellow lemons, two dishes containing soy sauce and two dishes of mignonette. Ben handed back his dish of soy and Carlos did the same.

When the fish platter was finished, the women returned with a wooden board arrayed with three cheeses, honey, nuts, champagne grapes and toasted bread rounds. They removed the soiled dishes from the fish course. The captain brought two glasses of Sauterne.

As they ate, the conversation was mostly about family, gardens and the sea.

Near the end of the cheese course, Y asked whether Ben's office was working on any new projects in Brazil. "Think of me if you are looking for investors."

"Thank you, Carlos, I will."

Ben wondered whether Bernadine might be the true source of the investment. He looked into Carlos' eyes, but it was Y's bright smile that answered the question.

"You will want to ask Mister Button if Spider might help you with Mister Stoekl." Y said this matter-of-factly, like he had asked to have the salt passed.

"Just 'Spider'."

"Yes, just 'Spider'."

BY THE TIME Ben arrived at his home high in the hills overlooking Grand Sac, Bill Button was on the veranda waiting for him. Bill was dressed in a white linen shirt and pleated khaki pants sans belt, his trouser cuffs rolled up exposing his ankles and boat shoe clad feet.

"Hello, Bill," Ben said, shaking Bill's hand vigorously. "Sorry for dragging you all the way to Saint Barth's, but I had another meeting here and wanted to meet somewhere that we could count on privacy."

"I see. Someone I know?"

"Carlos Y, but you knew that, didn't you?"

"Yes, but I wasn't sure that you wanted me to."

"Bill, I'll ask you a question: Can I trust you?"

"That's situational. I probably wouldn't kill you, but that may be situational too."

"If I ask you a direct question about Rachel, would you tell me the truth?"

"Probably."

"If I asked you a direct question about the night that we were ambushed in Lexington, would you answer me honestly?"

"Most likely."

"Will you introduce me to Spider?"

"No."

Ben waited as Bill searched his eyes looking for any information they might reveal.

Bill finally spoke. "Why would you ask me about Spider?"

"Because Carlos Y thinks that Spider might be useful in getting to Stoekl."

"While it's true that I have worked with Spider on three occasions, I have never met him."

"So, it's a him."

"Not necessarily. Spider has deep cover. I don't know who knows him, has met him or has any idea where he might be."

"Is he CIA or Treasury?"

"CIA. NCS. National Clandestine Service."

"He's a spy?"

"The best."

"Why would he know Stoekl?"

"I don't know. I don't really know Stoekl. At most, I've met him twice. Most of what I know about him I was told by Treasury."

"When did they tell you that he was a good guy?"

"The night of the ambush."

"Before or after?"

"Just as we were preparing to roll."

"So, you can contact this 'Spider'?"

"Yes."

"Can I talk to him...or her?"

"He'll decide that. We'll need to be specific regarding our need for him, what we want him to do and why he's the only guy who can do it."

"Okay. Here it is. First, I want to make sure that Stoekl knows that Dashkov is dead. I think that he most probably already knows, but there is someone or something keeping Stoekl, and therefore Piscara, in hiding. It might be Pierce, if he is in Dashkov's pocket, but it might be something else. Maybe Pierce is planning to take up where Dashkov left off. I—we—need to know so that we can solve the problem."

"How do you intend to solve the problem?"

Ben smiled. "That's situational."

TWO MORNINGS LATER, Ben left the house at 11 Sebastien Bottin and walked to the news dealer on Boulevard Raspail, near the Metro station. As he left the kiosk, he glanced across the intersection at Le Saint Germain café and the table that he and Pascal often shared. Their table was empty. Ben crossed the intersection, approached the café and settled in his seat.

"Ah, Monsieur Holt, it is good to see you again." Alain was Ben's usual waiter. He stood before Ben in his daytime dress of black slacks and vest over a freshly pressed white shirt. His hair was brown and slicked back with pomade. His nose was regally gallic. "We had feared you had become lost. Will Monsieur Satart be joining you?"

"Not today, Alain."

"Will you be having your usual?"

"Yes, please. Merci."

Ben unfolded his newspaper, *Paris d'Aujourdhui,* and read the story just below the fold. It told of the activities of the Russian mob in international finance, including a vignette on the erstwhile activities of one Anton Vasilevich Dashkov and his alleged murder at the hands of his former associates after he had gotten too ambitious for their tastes. His body was found on a Rio beach and his yacht was found drifting offshore. It had been apparently abandoned by its crew who were either collaborating with his killers or were as-yet unfound victims.

Ben smiled. He liked the twist that he had added himself, of the drifting abandoned yacht. It wouldn't take long for the TV news to pick up the story, including the "leaked" video purporting to show the drifting yacht. He wondered whether Satart Holt's model maker would recognize his handiwork.

Alain arrived with his allongé and tartine. As Ben spread butter on pieces of the toasted bread, he looked toward his office and thought of the easier days he seemed to have left behind. He desperately wanted them back. As the sun broke through the morning clouds and warmed his face, he resolved to make those days his again.

Then, for the first time in a long time, he rose from his chair, dropped a bill and a coin into the small tray, and walked to his office.

LATER THAT DAY, Ben called Bill Button. "Anything yet?"

"Not that I've heard, but that doesn't mean that nothing is happening."

"Can you be sure of that?"

"No."

64

EACH MORNING SINCE SEVERINE'S ARRIVAL, SHE, Claudine and Annie would sit in the garden and have breakfast while planning their day. Then they would take a short walk, at first only a block or so, and return so that Claudine could go to bed and rest.

After a couple of weeks of this routine, Severine suggested that they might get a cold tub for Claudine to soak in for a few moments after their walk. It sounded like torture to Ben and he winced at the thought, but Claudine wanted to try it. After a week, the cold baths proved to have worked miracles. Claudine was walking at least three blocks before returning for the ice bath. After that, she awoke each day excited to get out and walk.

AS EXCITED AS Claudine was, Ben was giving up hope that the Spider connection had any chance of ending Piscara's captivity. He decided to call Button and propose an alternate route. He would use his connections, with Marcel's support, to bring TRACFIN, the French government's anti-financial fraud unit, into the case.

He sat in the Library with the doors closed and lifted the receiver. He did not hear a dial tone. He was about to hang up and try again when he heard a voice.

"Hello?"

"Yes, who is this?"

"Am I talking to Ben Holt?"

"Who is this?"

"Am I talking to Ben Holt?" The voice was insistent.

"Yes, you are."

"I am John Stoekl and I have someone here who wants to talk to you."

"Okay. Shall I assume that it is Piscara?" There was no response. Instead there was along pause and some muffled conversation in the background. Then, the unmistakable voice of Dean Arcangelo Piscara commanded Ben's attention. "Holt, when will I see you? We can't sit around. We need to have a Board meeting tonight."

"Dean, where are you?"

"In my office. Where would you expect me to be?"

"I guess I don't know." Ben sat back so forcefully in his chair that he almost fell over backwards. He heard the voice in the earpiece but didn't hear the words for a very long moment.

When he finally recovered he realized that Dean Piscara was insisting that Ben set a Board meeting for that evening. Ben listened patiently until the old man stopped to take a breath, then pointed out that the by-laws required twenty-four hours notice. He would set the meeting for the next night.

"You wouldn't believe what I've learned over the last couple of days," Dean said. "Mister Stoekl has some pretty damning information that puts Mo Sather in a very poor light."

"Dean, let me ask you a question. How long have you been with Mister Stoekl?"

"Two or three days. Since you gave me a ride home."

"Good. Let me get the meeting called."

Ben hung up the phone realizing that his old friend was losing his mental acuity. Not unexpected, he thought, for a ninety-six year old man, but still worrisome for Ben.

BEN FLEW TO Boston the next afternoon, just after having lunch with Claudine. He planned to get the Board meeting over by nine p.m. Boston time and be back in Paris before lunch the next day.

PISCARA WAS SURPRISED, disappointed and quite angry that Sather was not at the Board meeting. He had intended to lecture Sather on his lack of loyalty to the institution and his failure to live up to the tenets of the BIA ideals. He repeatedly tried to make motions to that effect, but his words were garbled and his thoughts distracted. It was all that Ben could do to keep the meeting on track. Some of the discussion points raised by his fellow Board members were at least as nonsensical as Piscara's. It was only with Hezekiah Wilson's help that Ben was able to get the sole motion that he wanted and needed approved for the conclusion to the Sather affair.

In the end, the BIA Board voted that the property of the BIA was not for sale. As soon as the motion was passed, Ben gaveled the meeting to a close, fearing that any further discussion would just muddy the waters.

AFTER THE MEETING, Ben drove Piscara to the nursing home where Eda was now resident. His nephew was waiting for him, along with a doctor and a nurse. Ben didn't know it, but this was to be the last time he would see Piscara alive.

ON THE FLIGHT back to Paris, Ben realized for the first time that a great weight had been lifted from his shoulders. Piscara had been released from his captivity, although he wouldn't return to the BIA.

The process for picking a new Dean would not start while Piscara was alive—no one on the Board was willing to broach that subject. There were a lot of other loose ends and unanswered questions, but they really didn't bother Ben much.

What had become of Sather? Who was John Stoekl? Ben still hadn't met him. Where was Simon Pierce and what was his role in this whole mess?

Ben tallied the score and in the end was not very happy with the results. Piscara was back—sort of. The BIA was safe, at least for now. Strout was dead. Pascal Satart was gone. Still, he was alive and he had his family. Claudine was doing much better and a cure—or at least an effective treatment—was at hand.

He thought about the things that made his life normal. He took out his sketchpad and started a list. When he got back to Paris he would pay more attention of each of those things. On the top of the list was a single word: *flaneur*.

As Ben's plane approached Paris, the co-pilot told him there was a call for him on the new satellite phone. The phone had been given to him just after the Carmen Ortega interview at the Elysees Palace. It was a diplomatic phone and conversations were scrambled. Ben had thought of it as a gesture by the French government to affirm Ben's role as a diplomat. He had stored it in the pilot's locker just outside the cockpit.

The co-pilot showed Ben the button that would connect him to the call. Ben took the large cumbersome device and, holding it in front of his face, pushed the button and held the phone near his right ear. It was a long moment before he spoke. "Yes, this is Ben Holt."

The voice on the other end of the phone said something, but Ben couldn't make out the crackling electronic words. He tried to concentrate on hearing the words and realized he was talking to John Stoekl.

"Where are you, John?"

"I..can'n'nt...ell you...at."

"I see. Did Bill Button tell you that I wanted to talk to you?"

"Neg...g...tive. Spider...note."

"Well, I really only have two questions for you, although I'd really like to meet you and thank you."

"May...ee...day."

"Which day?"

"Some day."

"Okay."

"...your quest...t....t...n?"

"Why did you keep Piscara so long and why did you release him when and where you did?"

"...was con...rned...Pierce...Russian mob...r, name...Vitaly... kin...Menkin...fled U S...exico. He...used...name...on Peirce."

"Did you say that he's in Mexico?"

"No...now, prob...ly...rope."

"Eastern Europe?"

"No, Paris."

Ben realized it was going to be useless to continue to try to talk to Stoekl. He thanked him again and expressed his hope that they would meet. Realizing that Pierce's continued presence in Paris would be a threat to him and his family, he called Bill Button and arranged to meet him at the airport when he landed. Then he called Gunter, who had spent the better part of a month in Germany for some needed R and R with his large extended family. Together, Button, Gunter and Ben would draw up a plan to safeguard Ben's family and lure Pierce out.

BILL BUTTON HAD made it clear from the start that he was opposed to Ben's goal of drawing Simon Pierce out into the open. Bill had argued vociferously against Ben's plan. Ben refused to listen to Bill's arguments except where they involved operational details. His plan involved him making very public appearances in a series of events. He scheduled major speaking engagements like public forums followed by smaller events in places ranging from classrooms to wine bars. He thought that Pierce was unlikely to make a move at a large public event and that an attack at a smaller event was more likely. Bill and Gunter cautioned that they would need to be prepared for any contingency. They also worried that Ben's involvement in so many public events where security would be needed might cause mission fatigue and that the security staff would let their guard down.

At the end of one particularly contentious session, Bill asked, "Why would you want to be involved in anything like this? Let the flics find him. Stay home. Take care of your family."

"He is in Paris because he wants me. I'm not going to sit around in a fortress while he tries to find a way in."

"Then send your family away until this is over."

"There is no safer place than here. We are on a street that is easy to secure, we have a secure perimeter within a secure perimeter and all of the high points around us are under our control. A classic security arrangement." Ben looked to Gunter, who nodded.

"Then stay put," Bill said.

Ben continued, "Our only vulnerability is time. Eventually someone will make a mistake, get bored or complacent—or Pierce will get smart. No, I want to find him, draw him out, end this whole matter."

"What will you use for bait?"

"I've been thinking about that. After considering all of the options and ruling each out one-by-one, there is only one thing left on the table."

"You." Button's eyes widened. He shook his head.

"Yes."

"How?"

"If Pierce is smart—and we all think he is—he's not going to make any quick moves. He's going to be watching me, assessing my security, looking for a weak spot. I'm going to be going about my days in my usual way, although with additional security with one apparent weak spot. I expect that he'll be careful about assessing that weak spot when he finds it. He'll want to make sure it's not a trap. Of course, it will be a trap, but we've got to carefully camouflage that fact."

"Okay, what is the weak spot and how does the trap work?"

"We don't know yet. I'm still working on that. Gunter is my tester. It has to pass the Gunter test before it becomes operational."

"This better be good." Button was clearly skeptical.

BEN SAT AT his table in the Satarr Holt office and drew time dia-grams in his sketchbook. He thought that it would be important to design some variations into his schedule, but he wanted to have the variations be standardized so that his security detail would be ready for them. They would need to understand them by instinct, since he didr.'t want to take the chance that someone on his detail would reveal his plan—either inadvertently or otherw.se.

"Ben?"

"Yes, Josep?"

"Are you going to move to Pascal's table?"

"Not yet. It doesn't feel right yet. Do you know what I mean?"

"Yes, I think so, but I was wondering if we could use it to hold some drawing files. Since you won't be using it, I will tell the assistants to go ahead."

"Okay. Wait. On second thought, call Severine and ask if she wants to use it."

"As you wish."

Some things never change, Ben thought. He was still a disap-pointment to Josep. Ben recalled his first days working with Pascal. Josep—a small man with a outlandishly large head topped by a shock of sparse, unruly white hair—had been the head of the office staff then, as he still was now. In those days, Josep had seen Ben as one of the many young men—and an occasional, though rare, young woman—who came through the office studying under Pascal. They had all been classified in Josep's mind as the office *artistes*. They hadn't known how to put a building together and had no desire to learn. Josep had grudg-ingly accepted that Ben knew how to put a building together, but he had never acknowledged it.

65

SIMON PIERCE SAT ON THE EDGE OF THE SINGLE BED, disassembling his Glock. Cleaning his guns had become second nature to him, so much so that he didn't need to look at the gun to disassemble and reassemble it. The room around him was intensely monochromatic: white walls, white coverlet and sheets, white Formica locker at the foot of each of the four beds. Even the window frames were white. He had paid the attendant extra to avoid filling up the other beds as long as the hostel didn't get too busy. Pierce had registered as Perry Simon. He had the credentials in his stash of a half-dozen different identities that he kept in a hidden compartment behind the lining of his backpack. He also had two guns hidden in the base of the pack. The lead that lined the base added some weight, but the weight was still manageable and the lead allowed Pierce to slip through Customs without being discovered.

As he wiped each of the parts with an oily rag, he pondered his next move. It would have to happen soon; things were getting hot around him. When he'd read of the discovery of Dashkov's body, he knew he had limited options. He could try to outrun his pursuers and make a run for Russia, but his phone calls to some of Dashkov's "investors" had proven fruitless. They all wanted to place some distance between themselves and the Boston dealings. He found that Dashkov's powerful friends might still be powerful, but they weren't committed to any friendship with their partner.

His wife still lived in Hong Kong, but she thought that he was an accountant for an American oil company. She was a good girl and the sex was good when he was home, but it wasn't actually love. He had used her as cover, just as he had used so many others. He wondered how many people he could count as true friends: perhaps his brother, but he had used him, too, and his identity was among those in his pack. "John Daniels," his passport read. He had used the joke of being "Jack Daniels" to spin his way through sticky situations with border guards and street cops. His mother had named him "Sam" because that was the name of the man she thought might be his father. He'd stolen the name "Simon Pierce" from a Vermont glassmaker and slightly modified the spelling of Pearce's last name.

He smiled when he thought of the biggest scam he'd had in a life chock-full of scams. He had convinced the Treasury Department that he was a graduate of MIT's Sloan School and the Kennedy School at Harvard. As it turned out, there had been a graduate from that joint program named Neil Simon Pierce. He had told them he'd hated the name Neil and hence only used his middle and last names. They'd laughed about the Neil Simon moniker and wondered if his mother had stalked the playwright. In his affable way, he had laughed with them. Amidst the laughter, they seemed to have missed the fact the Neil Simon Pierce was dead, killed in a car accident only weeks after graduation. The sad story had been a page one article in the Boston Globe.

After he had cleaned and reassembled his gun, Pierce pulled the black turtleneck and black pants from his pack. Once dressed, he walked to the polished steel full-length mirror near the door and looked himself over. The blackness stood out against the white room. Where he was going, the blackness would blend into the scruffy, dirty background. It would give him a temporary advantage against his target and his opponents. That's all he really wanted—enough time to kill Holt. He had no plan for escape, at least not in the temporal sense. He was ready for the ultimate escape and he had readied himself for it.

Pierce slipped down the back stairway. The alarm would sound when he opened the door, but it didn't matter. By the time the staff got to the door he would be long gone. He stopped at the landing at the bottom of the stairs, adjusted his black leather pack and stepped to the door, opening it with a quick, decisive move forward. He stopped when the alarm didn't sound, confused, and then shrugged and walked toward the Metro. Thirty yards later, he heard the alarm. He wondered if the staff had rigged it up on a time-delay, knowing that guests would use the door despite the alarm, but knowing they'd be happy if the door closed before the alarm sounded.

At the Metro station entry, Pierce paused to look at the kiosk bearing a map of the area and, on another of its three sides, a map of the Paris Metro system. He confirmed the stations where he would change lines and the station that was closest to his destination. He had two stops to make before he reached his final destination—one to pick up the car he had stashed in the garage below Rue de Bac and one more to pick up his bait.

AFTER THREE WEEKS of following his plan without any results, Ben was getting impatient for something to happen. Despite urging patience on others, he was beginning to consider abandoning his plan.

Following the schedule, Ben left the Saint Germain and headed back to his office. As he entered the stairway from the courtyard, he heard a woman sobbing near the top floor. When he heard her speak to someone, he realized that the sobs were coming from Lorraine, the office bookkeeper. When he reached the top of the stairs, he found a gathering that appeared to be most of the office staff. "What is going on?" he said.

"Oh, Monsieur Holt, it is terrible. A man with a gun came and took Monsieur Rufi." Lorraine now sobbed uncontrollably.

"Okay. Please calm down. Did the man ask for me?"

"No, he asked for Monsieur Rufi."

"Monsieur Rufi by name, or Josep?"

"Monsieur Rufi."

Peter, one of the young Americans working in the office raised his hand from behind Gustav, an older draftsman. "I didn't see a gun."

Several other voices from the crowd spoke up. "No, no gun."

"Lorraine, are you sure you saw a gun?" Ben asked.

Lorraine sobbed again, louder this time.

Ben reached out with both hands and laid them gently on her shoulders. "Lorraine?"

"I don't know. Maybe he *said* he had a gun."

"What did he look like?"

"An American, I think. Very tall. Taller than you. Very commanding."

Gustav spoke. "Very German. Yes, very commanding."

Peter offered, "He had no German accent. He was definitely American."

A voice from the back of the crowd: "Or Canadian."

Peter again: "He didn't act Canadian."

Gustav: "He acted German."

Ben raised his open palms in a signal to stop. "Did he say where he was taking Josep?"

Peter said, "He said that they would be among the ghosts. An odd thing to say, don't you think?"

Gustav: "Maybe he's taking Josep to a cemetery. What a terrible place to die. The Germans did that."

"Thank you all. Let's close the office for the day. I'm sure that Josep will be all right. Go home and tomorrow we may have some good news."

Slowly the small crowd broke up and went to their desks to gather their belongings.

"Peter," Ben said. He held up his hand to stop the young draftsman. "Before you go, please bring me the plans for the abandoned Metro stations, especially Saint-Martin and Champs de Mars."

Peter hesitated for a moment, then his face brightened. "The ghost stations! You think he took Josep to one of the ghost stations."

"Perhaps. Please bring me the plans."

"Yes, Ben."

66

B EN CALLED BILL BUTTON AND TOLD HIM OF JOSEP'S abduction and his plan to find and free him. He asked Lorraine to send Gunter up on her way out. Within half an hour, the three men stood around Ben's table and looked over the plans of the "Ghost Stations"—five in all.

Ben pointed out that some preparation work had started on two of the stations, Saint-Martin in the tenth arrondissement and Champs de Mars in the seventh, near the Eiffel Tower. The others were still boarded up. While it was possible that Pierce had taken Josep to one of the boarded up stations, Ben's bet was that they were at one of these two. He suggested that Bill and one of Gunter's people take Champs de Mars and that he and Gunter take Saint-Martin. Gunter would inform the Gendarmes of the situation, but only as they entered the stations, giving Ben's teams fifteen minutes or so to locate Pierce, and, hopefully, Josep. They would coordinate entry at exactly fifteen-thirty.

THE OLD SAINT-MARTIN Metro was the largest of the abandoned stations for which Satart Holt designed new uses and a new life. Both Saint-Martin and Champs de Mars were to be new nightclubs. The new uses for the other stations hadn't been decided, although one was likely to become a swimming club. Saint-Martin was, appropriately enough, on Boulevard Saint-Martin close to Saint-Martin's Gate. It had been closed since before the Second World War and had remained mostly untouched, except for the markings of graffiti artists. It held a treasure of old subway advertising posters, most spared by the artists.

When they arrived at the almost hidden entry to the station, Gunter drove the Suburban onto the sidewalk and used the truck to push away some pallets of brick that were to be used on the sidewalks outside the station and that were partially blocking the entry.

"I want to make sure that the Gendarmes see the entry."

"I'm hoping that this will be the end of this crazy situation, Gunter."

"Yes, sir, but let's be careful. Pierce wants this to be the end of you."

"I know, but I don't understand why. The game was over when Dashkov died... why continue to play it out?"

"Maybe you'll learn that if we take Pierce alive."

"Let me go in first."

"Okay, but I'll be right behind you."

"Five minutes."

"Three." Gunter said.

Gunter took a Beretta from the shoulder holster under his jacket. He handed it to Ben, then reached over and flipped off the safety. He reached under his jacket at the waist and removed a Glock, again flipping the safety. He nodded to Ben who handed him a cellphone. Gunter looked at his watch, then called a private number to talk to an old friend, a Gendarme Captain. He told him a short version of the story, mentioned Ben's name and then touched the phone's off button without saying goodbye.

"You didn't say goodbye to the captain." Ben took the phone from Gunter.

"No. Bad luck."

"Okay, let's go."

"No one would blame you for waiting here, Ben."

"I would."

Gunter cracked a small smile and watched Ben enter the subway and disappear into its darkness. He stared at the large hand on his watch waiting for it to move. "Come on, come on!" He whispered to the large hand, urging it to move. One click. At least he knew it was working, he thought. Two clicks. "Good, good. Let's go!" When it moved three clicks, he took a deep breath and entered the subway.

Meanwhile, Ben had descended the dark stairs carefully. The bare construction bulbs were dark, either because Pierce had turned them off or because a construction worker had done so when they were leaving for the day. In either case, the darkness was welcoming. He didn't want to be a lighted target.

Ben saw that there was a pool of light at the bottom of the stairs where they met the passageway that extended under the road above. When he reached the passageway, he stopped, flattened himself against the wall for protection and peered along the three tunnels that led to the platform levels and to another exit. He knew that each of the tunnels had cross-tunnels and a warren of small rooms off of them that might make for good hiding places for Pierce.

As he was carefully advancing down the central corridor, he heard the bleat of sirens from the street above. The Gendarmes were early.

He reached the end of the corridor and emerged onto the platform hall, a hall that was full of staging from the floor to the ceiling in the area where the tracks had been. The edges of the hall—an area ten feet wide along the platform area—were free of staging.

BEN SAW MOVEMENT along the platform near where a right-hand tunnel emerged into the hall some fifty yards away. He instinctively flattened himself against the wall and raised his gun to shoulder level in a two-hand grip. Then he saw that the moving figure was Gunter. He watched as Gunter bent over the form of a man propped against a wall. When the man stood, Ben's spirits rose.

Gunter waved to Ben, and Ben waved back. He was about to head toward Gunter and Josep when he realized that Gunter was not waving him forward, but was waving him back and pointing toward the opposite corner of the station, to the left and slightly behind Ben. Ben turned and saw a shadowy figure raise his arm.

Too late for him to move to cover, he heard the crack of a gunshot. It echoed in the hall. He felt a burning pain in his chest. The pain was white hot. He heard garbled voices—some electronic—and several more gunshots. He struggled to remain standing, leaning back against the wall for support. He was determined not to lose consciousness, but his legs couldn't hold him and he slumped to the floor.

CLAUDINE WAS SMILING at him, and the children—all except Abeille—were wrestling Ben to the ground. Daniel was there with his arms around Ben's chest. Abeille sat beside the entwined bodies, happily clapping. Claudine walked over to the garden table, poured a glass of water and brought it to Ben. It was sunny and warm, the strong morning light shining in Ben's eyes. Then he thought that this was odd. They were in the shady part of the garden. The scene started getting smaller. Blackness closed in and all was gone.

67

I T HAD BEEN JUST OVER TWO YEARS SINCE BEN HAD
been shot by Simon Pierce in the Saint-Martin ghost station. Soon,
the station would be a ghost no longer. It would be reborn as a night-
club and restaurant—the work of Josep and Severine—with more than
enough interference from Ben. It was to be called "BH" and would be
decorated with sketches and model fragments from Ben's work. The ta-
blecloths and linens would be of an earth tone dyed linen, a contribution
from Claudine. It had been her last project. The dinnerware would be a
pure white, to set off the color of the linens.

BEN WAS LYING on his back in bed, his eyes closed, his hands tucked
behind his head. He sensed movement in the room and opened his eyes
just as the bright summer sun hit his face. He strained to open his eyes
but only managed a painful squint. He wondered what day it was. It felt
like a Tuesday, but he wasn't sure. It was the painkillers, he knew. They
helped him sleep, but they confused him when he awoke.

The form at the tall windows—clearly a woman—moved from one
window to the next, drawing aside the heavy drapes, fastening a chord
to the jamb, then drawing aside the gauzy curtain.

"Good morning, Ben. The children are all up and eating breakfast."

"Can you ask Babette to send up my tartine? I want to sit on the balcony for a bit before we go for our *flaneur*."

"I will, and I'll tell the children that you'll be down after meditation."

"Thank you, Annie."

ANNIE TOOK CARE of Ben. After Claudine's death, Ben had lost his will to do the difficult exercises required for his rehabilitation. Annie stayed beside him during the visits with the therapist and helped him with the regimen designed to help him first sit up, then stand with assistance to move into a wheelchair, and eventually walk—albeit with great difficulty. There had been long, frustrating sessions that ended with Ben cursing the therapist and Annie for forcing him to continue despite the pain, but he loved Annie for her efforts, and he loved her for her kindness to Claudine during the long, difficult months she had cared for her before her death.

CLAUDINE HAD DIED in Ben's arms when they were the only part of his body he could move. He had rubbed her back during her final moments, listening as her breaths became shallower and harder to hear. She had passed away just as the morning sun rose above the nearby rooftops, illuminating the faces of her children sitting at the edge of the bed. Annie had been at her head, checking the pulse in her neck occasionally, and Severine had been at the foot of the bed, rubbing Claudine's feet.

BEN BEGAN EVERY day the same way—meditation followed by his breakfast of tartine and allongé. In the past, his morning meditations had been aimed at clearing his mind. Now he found it impossible to live without spending some time with Claudine's spirit each morning. Severine was understanding, though Ben expected he would need to give up these moments once they were married. She wouldn't ask that of him, but it felt like a betrayal of her trust and love. They often talked about Pascal and Claudine, shared stories about each of them, and agreed that—while they needed to bring to their relationship a commitment to each other—Pascal and Claudine would always be a part of their lives.

BEN HAD PLANNED to take a trip to Rio as soon as he was able to travel. He hadn't told Severine, but he'd wanted to ask her very traditional father for Severine's hand in marriage. His plans fell apart when Severine casually asked him—at breakfast one Sunday morning—if he had any plans for that afternoon.

"Nothing specific. Why?" Ben didn't look up from the newspaper he was reading until Abeille started giggling.

"Because we thought it might be a nice day for a wedding." Severine had her arms around Emma and Abeille. Ben wanted to protest that he already had a plan, but the three smiles facing him made him realize that his plans were not important. He smiled and nodded. The three women broke into a song and danced happily around the courtyard. Ben looked at his daughters, then at Severine, so young and so beautiful. "Three sisters", he thought and smiled broadly.

Ben called Daniel and Pascha. Severine called Marcel. The whole family—including Annie, Robert and Babette—got dressed up and went out to the rose garden at Jardin Saint-Gilles-Grand-Veneur together. There Severine and Ben were married by the Mayor of Paris.

SEVERINE AND THE boys—Daniel and Pascha—had reopened Claudine's atelier and had put on a wonderful show of Claudine's work during Fashion Week. Severine was at Satart Holt four days a week, so

Daniel ran the business side of the fashion house while Pascha ran the creative side. He was so young—but so natural—that Marcel claimed that he had channeled his mother's natural sense of fashion.

Daniel's girlfriend, Simone, was expecting a baby soon and Ben had hopes that they would marry before the child was born, but Severine counseled Ben not to press the issue.

BEN SPENT AS much time as he could over the last several months as father and mother to his family, especially to Emma and Abeille. He spent two mornings a week at Satart Holt, but always had lunch at the Saint-Germain with his daughters when they were not in school.

By spring, Ben was out of the motorized wheelchair. He was able to walk, sometimes without support, but rather slowly. Annie knew that Ben was still in quite a bit of pain, but he refused to give up *flaneur* and, if he walked somewhat slowly, this was the perfect pace for *flaneur*.

THE CHILDREN LOVED Annie, and Ben hoped she would stay to help with the girls after the wedding. She was spending a lot of time with Diane and Josh, and her daughter, Liz, who had moved to Paris to work for Marcel.

MARCEL HAD AGED considerably since Claudine's death and seemed to suddenly become frail. Severine had suggested that Ben spend more time with him, and he did. Their regular breakfast get-togethers began to include a few other older men, and Marcel seemed to regain some of his drive because of it. He, Ben and the others began mentoring young men and women who were just starting out in business. The group shared insights and advice, and occasionally a small investment.

They called themselves "Le Vieux Hommes Fous," and while they may have been old, they were definitely not crazy. They christened Ben their guardian.

JOSH AND HIS team had perfected the delivery system for the cancer radiation system. The clinical trials were going well, but it would be a few years before the system was fully approved. Then there would be the campaign to get the health system to pay for it.

BEN'S CONFINEMENT IN Paris meant he had almost no involvement in the life of the BIA. Ben had hoped that Hezekiah Wilson might succeed him, but Wilson hadn't shared Ben's belief that he'd be the perfect leader for the school. Wilson continued on the Board, but preferred to be a quiet voice. His strategy may have been brilliant because, from his post as Chair of the Education Committee, he was able to shepherd many of Ben's program initiatives into existence.

THERE WAS TALK about the need to appoint a new Dean, but nothing came of it. The older members of the Board couldn't think of anyone being Dean other than Piscara. It wasn't a question of credentials or experience. Piscara himself had neither of those when he was appointed Dean so many years earlier. They could find someone to do the job, but there could never be anyone to *be* the Dean.

CARLOS Y WAS shot to death in the café where he and Ben had met. The gunman had been one of his bodyguards.

MISSUS PITTSFIELD WAS beaten to death in her home by the drug-addict boyfriend of her daughter. She had refused to give him money to pay his dealer.

CAROL LAPIERRE HAD heeded her friends' warnings and given up one-night stands. She had settled down with one of the design studio instructors until she found out his long absences on lecture tours were actually trips home to his wife and children in Madison, Wisconsin. After she learned of his other life, Carol declared her intention to give up men—and sex.

BILL BUTTON SOBBED uncontrollably at the wedding of his daughter, Amélie. Ben looked for the face of her mother, Rachel, in the crowd, but didn't see her. He was sure that she and Bernadine had not died on the missing plane.

68

THE GONG THAT MARKED THE END OF BEN'S MEDITA-
tion was the signal to the children that Ben was available and
Abeille was the first to rush to his lap.

"You are certainly a speedy little bee, Abeille."

"I was hiding behind the door, Da-dee." Abeille giggled and her
light filled Ben's heart.

"And being so quiet, not even a buzzzzz." Ben kissed her forehead.

"Can you tell me another story about Claudine?"

"Well, let's see. Did I tell you the story of how we met?"

"Yes, Da-dee, but please tell me again." Abeille turned in Ben's lap
and held his face in her little hands. Ben was smitten. He coughed a
single cough to regain his composure.

"Well, I had just arrived in Paris and Oncle Pascal invited me to
a party..."

Acknowledgements

I WANT TO THANK TIM HUGGINS FOR HIS ON-GOING and insightful advice and Rebecca Boyd, my editor, for her strong hand and her willingness to endure my grumbling. They made this book much better.

I need to thank Klaudia Mally and Carri Wroblewski of Brix Wine Shop in Boston and Nantucket for teaching me about great wines, good food and their central role in the life of friendships.

Finally, to my late friend Isabelle Deschamps Fontaine: I miss you, but hope that you have found the peace that eluded you in life.

About the Author

GLENN MORRIS IS AN ARCHITECT WHO LIVES JUST A short trip down the Massachusetts Turnpike from Boston. When he's in Boston, he dreams of being in Paris again. When he's in Paris, he dreams of being in Paris again.

Mr. Morris taught architecture and design for more than 25 years and was the founder and Chair of the College of Interior Design at the Boston Architectural College. He was formerly Chair of the Newton (MA) Urban Design Commission and currently serves on the Boards of Regis College and St. Mary's High School in Lynn, MA.

He is the chairman of Morris Architects, an architecture and interior design firm specializing in commercial and business design, and Strategic Facilities Partners, owners' project managers.

His next Ben Holt novel, *A Foundation of Ghosts*, is gestating.

About Paris

There are no words to express the sadness and anger that we feel about the tragic events of 13 November 2015.

#prayforparis

www.ingramcontent.com/pod-product-compliance
Lightning Source LLC
Chambersburg PA
CBHW051246260626
47162CB00002B/628